C000179469

Beyond Limits
(The Afterlife Series Book 5)
By Deb McEwan

Copyright © Deb McEwan 2020
All rights reserved
ISBN 978-9925-7702-0-5

The right of Deb McEwan to be identified as
the author of this work has been asserted by her in
accordance with the Copyright, Designs and Patents
Act 1988.
This is a work of fiction. While some places and
events are a matter of fact, the characters are the
product of the author's imagination and are used in a
fictitious manner. Any resemblance to actual persons,
living or dead, is purely coincidental.

Cover Design by Jessica Bell

For the dead who are still with us

Author's Note

Thanks for choosing 'Beyond Limits', Book Five in my Afterlife Series. If you haven't read the first four books ('Beyond Death', 'Beyond Life', 'Beyond Destiny', and 'Beyond Possession') I recommend you read them before this one. Here's a summary of the story so far:

Big Ed has coerced three teenage girls into accompanying him to a party with the offer of free food and booze. They're unaware they will be groomed to have sex with older men. Melanie smells a rat, changes her mind and leaves the car before it reaches its destination.

Claire Sylvester dies in an RTA the morning after the best night of her life, along with Ron, her taxi driver. Her twin brothers Tony and Jim know she's dead before being told.

An angel named Gabriella tell Claire and Ron there's a backlog of souls waiting to be processed due to a natural disaster on earth. They're kept at Cherussola until the Committee decides their future but are allowed to visit their friends and family. Claire discovers that her fiancée had a one-night stand with her best friend and that her parents' marriage is a sham. Her father has been living a double life for many years and she has a half-sister called Melanie. She also discovers she can communicate with her brothers and that she has powers that many dead souls do not.

Ron discovers his wife had an affair with Ken, his former boss. Ken dies and goes to Hell. He is reincarnated in different forms and his soul is in constant fear and pain.

Claire's mother, Marion, and Ron's wife, Val, meet by chance and join a charity. At a get-together, Tony meets Val's daughter, Libby; they become romantically involved.

Val is already in a delicate state due to her husband's death. She is mugged (by three humans and one evil soul) during a training course and Ron begs Claire to do everything in her power to bring the muggers to justice. They discover where the muggers live and hang out, then hatch a clever plan to catch them, involving Claire's twin brothers and Jim's girlfriend, Fiona.

Melanie's friends tell her about their ordeal, so she informs the police. Big Ed and his accomplice, Sandy, kidnap her. Claire helps her brothers to find and save Melanie, but Big Ed escapes, along with Sandy. He loses his temper and kills Sandy.

Having observed Claire and Ron's work with the twins, the Committee informs Gabriella that Claire is to remain where she is for a while to help people while the angels are busy dealing with the backlog. Ron has the choice of whether to remain with Claire or to move on to eternity. Claire is sent back to Earth to visit her family and friends, not knowing whether Ron will be in Cherussola when she returns.

On her pleasant journey upwards, Sandy feels a rough jolt. The Committee have decided that she was complicit in Big Ed's crimes so must go to Hell. The decision causes a disagreement and Gabriella's brother is removed from the Committee by his mother, Amanda.

Sandy suffers torture, and humiliation in Hell but refuses to cooperate with the demons. They return her to Earth to suffer in many different guises. The Committee eventually relent and save her between reincarnations.

Unable to return to Cherussola, Claire spends time watching her family and friends. Tony and Libby marry in Gretna Green while their mothers are in Zambia, working in an orphanage for their charity. When Gabriella returns Claire to Cherussola, she introduces her to Sandy. Ron decides he wants to stay with Claire and look out for his wife Val, so delays his journey to heaven. Claire ensures that Libby knows her father watched her wedding.

Big Ed, now calling himself Gary, has fled the country and had cosmetic surgery to alter his looks. He is still supplying men with young girls but has a legitimate building business for cover. Marion and Val meet him while in Zambia. Val is instantly attracted to him, but Marion has a bad feeling – the women fall out, but Marion's instincts prove to be correct. Girls go missing from the orphanage; some presumed dead from animal attacks.

Claire meets the angel Raphael who is Gabriella's twin. The attraction is mutual.

Claire's father, Graham, overcomes his many problems and turns his life around by becoming a bodybuilder. His ex-girlfriend, Carol, softens, and they eventually get back together.

Claire has a near miss and is saved from Hell by Raphael, Gabriella and some others. Back home, Gabriella explains that Claire is being recruited to help the fight against evil. She explains how some evils are contained in a hard-to-access cave known by the locals as Hell on Earth. A number of evil souls in the guise of cockroaches are watched over by angels, disguised as bats.

Jim and Fiona marry and Tony and Libby receive a blessing at the same time.

With help from the angels and spirits, Big Ed is eventually caught and jailed for his heinous crimes. He meets an untimely death in a foreign prison and is sent to Hell.

Claire, her angel lover Raphael, and his mother try to avoid Hell's gates while fighting the demons. While they are preoccupied, serpents amass outside the cave known as Hell on Earth.

Val is depressed and struggles to come to terms with the humiliation and shame of being involved with Big Ed, who she knows as Gary. She starts to self-harm, then attempts suicide.

Gabriella mounts a rescue mission to bring back her mother, brother and Claire from the gates of Hell.

The angels are busy, and the evils take advantage. Evils are sent to the cave known as Hell on Earth in the form of serpents, to release other evil souls from their prison. While many evils are at the cave working on the escape, the angel Zach is able to escape from Hell. He meets Claire and the others involved in the rescue attempt. Claire is ordered to return to Cherussola with Zach, while Gabriella and the host attempt to rescue her mother and brother.

Harry, Big Ed's son, escapes from the cave. He needs help to avenge the wrongs against him so goes in search of his father.

After a number of reincarnations as a lap dog, the evils eventually claim Big Ed. He is taken to his rightful home in Hell. After his initiation, his masters recognise him as one of their own and realise his strength. Some try to get on his side, knowing it's only a matter of time before he becomes their superior. When he's strong enough, he punishes those who tortured him when he first arrived.

The twins are headhunted by the staff from the secret school for people with special abilities (SAP School). They are recruited and have to pretend they work for a different organisation.

Big Ed is determined to seek revenge against a number of people still living. He meets with Harry and issues orders. Harry obeys without question, knowing his son will eventually become more powerful. Until he does, Big Ed has to carry out menial tasks to learn his trade and to build his strength.

Marion dreams that Melanie is attacked. She visits Carol and they hear Melanie scream. They rush her to hospital after she is attacked by a vicious, otherworldly spider. Past events are put to bed as Marion forgives Carol and becomes close to Melanie, Claire's half-sister.

Though still in pain, Raphael notices his torture is now random. He is able to look around and realises a number of senior evils are missing. His mother transmits her thoughts, telling him it is time to escape. They do so, taking some misplaced good souls with them.

Following selection, Tony and Jim carry out various roles for the school. Their wives are suspicious, more so Fiona, who is eventually recruited.

When Marion and Libby go to collect Val from hospital, they meet her psychiatrist, Dr Basil Walters. This is life changing for Marion and the doctor.

Claire has to decide how to fight the evils, not knowing whether the other angels will return. Zach wakes up and, although he is a senior angel, it is obvious that his time in Hell has affected him. Claire notices his scars and broken body. She formulates a plan to help fight the evils and recruits Ron and Sandy. Zach is not back to full fitness and can only give limited assistance.

Raphael returns to Claire, broken. He sleeps for what seems like an eternity and she wonders if he will ever wake up.

Graham travels to weight-lifting competitions so Marion spends more time with Carol and Melanie. Val believes that Gary is visiting her dreams and Libby discovers this when she rooms with her mother during one of Mel's visits.

The Committee is too busy to hear Claire's ideas, so she decides to go ahead with her plan, without their permission.

Various attempts to discover details about the SAP School are thwarted. The twins' training is intensified as the staff want to know whether their communications with their dead sister could assist in the fight against crime.

The evils are becoming more organised and are starting to win the battle against good.

After a period of peace, Val's nightmares return and become worse. She knows that Gary is in her head when she's asleep. As well as being terrified, it's driving her insane.

Marion has a secret relationship with Basil, not yet ready to tell her family about him. While she's away, Melanie has nightmares involving Big Ed.

Big Ed practises his possession techniques. Once he's satisfied he can overcome any hosts, he sets out to find an evil person who he can bring into line.

Claire has a run-in with an evil known as Goth, who later escapes. When they next meet, she transforms Goth's body into a cockroach. Goth has arranged a surprise for Claire's brothers, so Claire has to leave her before being able to transform her head.

Big Ed possesses mad Martin, the country's most notorious serial killer, during a prison transfer. He escapes and commits further murders. Eventually, Big Ed dominates him, and he is forced to go along with his plans. Big Ed, now in the body of Mad Martin goes to claim Val.

Gabriella and Amanda return to work and Claire is promoted to angel while on a mission. With Gabriella's help, they find Goth-Roach, turn her head into a roach, and deliver her to the cave.

Claire sleeps on return to Cherussola and is awoken by Raphael. He is scarred and damaged but is going to get better.

Claire, Gabriella, Raphael, Zach and Ron watch as Mad Martin heads for Marion's apartment, buoyed on by the voice in his head. Val is home alone as he enters the house and makes his way to her bedroom. When he speaks, Val knows that Gary has taken over his mind and body. He walks toward her carrying a knife and she backs towards the window. Opening it, she climbs out onto the ledge. He joins her and Val embraces him, then jumps. Libby and Tony pull up in their car in time for Libby to see her mother and the man landing on the concrete.

As Claire is transforming Big Ed, a dark invisible presence arrives and drags him and Mad Martin away. The Devil doesn't show himself but torments the souls until they can take no more. He then shows himself and destroys them permanently. When he'd finished with them, the Devil turns to Claire and undresses her with his eyes, before putting a hand on her shoulder and pushing her downwards. He starts to torture her as he pushes her further down towards his home. As she loses hope, Claire hears the voice of the Lord. She feels warmth on her body and the Devil's mark disappears from her shoulder.

The Lord and Devil fight until the Devil returns to Hell with his tail between his legs, vowing to win the next round.

When trying to give the recently deceased Val a second chance at life, an angel makes a mistake causing the soul of a child to be suspended in the ether where she floats aimlessly, believing she's dreaming.

A natural disaster causes a fissure in the cave known as hell on earth. By the time the guards realise what's happened, it's too late to recapture the evil souls who have escaped. Two escapees, Goth-Roach and Harry, are the former enemies of Claire and her family. They find the young child's soul and are determined to groom her, so she can carry out the devil's work.

While Claire's twin brothers, Tony and Jim, are learning to enhance their telepathic abilities at the

SAP School, Libby, Tony's wife, is unable to come to terms with the death of her mother and seeks solace elsewhere. She meets Cassie, who murders her – Libby is eventually reincarnated, and Cassie is punished for her crimes.

The Devil's servants torment dead souls by returning them to earth in various guises. They also arrange for a number of children to be possessed so they can carry out evil deeds. Chaos ensues as stories of children committing heinous crimes grab the media's attention. The twins attempt to contact their dead sister, Claire, for help, but she doesn't respond.

Souls are stolen from both sides as the battle between good and evil persists.

Goth-Roach has ambitious plans to exact revenge on Claire by destroying the angel and her family, and to increase her standing with the Devil, but her plan doesn't work. She's transformed and banished to the cave.

Ron and Sandy are eventually reunited, in a good place. Claire's mum saves the life of Mel (Claire's half-sister) and marries Basil.

And now book five...

Chapter 1 – The Present

Claire loved being an angel. If all went to plan, she wouldn't be able to visit her twin brothers, Jim and Tony, for quite some time and she wanted them to know they'd be on their own for a while. She also had a message for them both, so she decided to give them a quick heads-up before returning to her soulmate, Raphael, and a mission that she'd desired for almost as long as she'd been an angel.

She decided to visit Tony first. The moon was glinting through a gap in the curtains as Claire looked down on her brother who was crashed out on his settee in the living room. He was fully clothed, snoring loudly, and face down with one arm dangling near an empty wine bottle. Claire knew he sometimes had trouble sleeping since Libby's murder, but was still surprised to see him in this state. She summoned some extra energy, brought a lightweight quilt from the spare room and placed it over him.

'Tony,' she called. 'Tony, I need to speak to you.'

Her only answer was a loud snore, so Claire looked around for a sturdy ornament. She found a wooden elephant on a bookshelf and willed it to the coffee table. Tapping the elephant on the table, she gradually increased the force until something seeped into his subconscious and Tony sat up.

'You shouldn't drink so much,' Claire said. 'What if I was an intruder?'

Tony yawned and rubbed his eyes, not surprised to hear his dead sister's voice. 'I hate to put too fine a point on it, Claire, but you are an intruder.'

'You know what I mean,' she replied. 'I wanted to let you know that you're going to be working from Oxford Street in the not too distant future.'

'Oxford Street? In London? We're moving again?' Tony sat up and shook his head, trying to take in her words and clear the alcohol from his brain.

'Yes, Tony, to London.'

'But why, what's happening and why…?'

'I can't explain now. You'll find out before too long, but I won't be back for some time so you and Jim will need to look out for yourselves and the others. There's trouble brewing. We don't have all the details yet, but be vigilant and careful around strangers, and trust your gut. If it doesn't feel right…'

'Yes, Claire. Can I go back to sleep now?'

'Take care, Tony, and try to be kinder to yourself.'

'It was a one-off, Claire. We're all entitled to overdo it every now and then…' He stopped, knowing she'd already left. Tony smiled to himself when he realised that his sister must have put the quilt over him, and he knew she was right; he *was* drinking too much, but it helped him to sleep when he had lots on his mind, the job as well as Libby.

He yawned and stretched. *Maybe I should get Spike back from Mum's*, he thought, missing the company of his dog. It was difficult when he was often away on missions, but Tony knew he'd drink less if he wasn't so lonely and had Spike to think about. He went to the kitchen and downed a glass of water, returned the quilt to the spare room, then went to his bedroom, undressed, and slept in a haze of alcohol.

It was a different story at her other brother's. Claire smiled at the sight of Jim and his wife Fiona spooned together in their king-sized bed. Jim's eyelids were flickering and one of his arms was twitching. Recognising the REM stage of sleep, Claire knew she'd be able to pass the message without having to wake him.

'Oxford Street,' she said.

'Ugh?' he grunted.

'Your new place of work is going to be Oxford Street, but not for a while yet. Okay?'

'Okay,' Jim said clearly.

'And keep an eye on Tony. He's not himself and I'm worried about him.'

'I know and I got it,' said Jim.

'Go away, Claire. It's the middle of the night and we're trying to sleep,' said Fiona, without opening her eyes.

'Remember what I said, Jim,' she told her brother as a parting shot before disappearing.

*****

In one of the worlds inhabited by dead souls, the sound of groaning woke Ron from a deep sleep. He shook himself as he looked at the face glaring at him from above.

'I know you're not Ron,' she said. 'You can't trick me again. Leave me alone. Just leave me alone...' She screamed, shaking her head violently. Then her expression changed as the anger left and Ron saw the fear in her eyes before she closed them and shuddered, dropping down next to him. She then put her hands over her face and cried.

It sounded to Ron as if the world was coming to an end. It took him a moment to realise he wasn't dreaming, and that the angels must have rescued Sandy from Hell. He sat up quickly and put his arms around her. She was shivering like a puppy rescued from icy waters but didn't fight him off. He made soothing noises, like he had when his daughter Libby woke from a nightmare, and felt her shivers calming in his arms.

'Is it really you, Ron?'

'Yes, my love. It's really me. The angels have brought you back.'

'Oh, Ron...'

3

He felt her grip on him tighten as she held him and sobbed her heart out. She was damaged but Ron hoped time would heal the wounds. He knew he wouldn't be able to visit earth with her again – there was no way Sandy could cope with any chance encounters with evils and the possibility of being dragged back to Hell would tip the balance and drive her insane.

As he pondered her future, the Committee was doing exactly the same.

*****

'So it's agreed that it's time?' asked Amanda.

Although the opinions of Martin and the others were important to her, she looked to her children, Gabriella and Raphael, and Raphael's soul mate, Claire, for input. They knew Ron and Sandy the best, and if anybody had an opinion, she knew it would be Claire.

'Do we tell him about Libby?' Claire asked.

Always a difficult question and no less of a dilemma just because it had happened many times before. After leaving her husband, Tony, for another woman, Libby had been murdered. Her actions had been far less than perfect and, unbeknown to her, she'd been given another chance to prove herself. Now known as Maria Wong, she'd already been placed with a new family and was doing well, though still a baby; so it was early days. Her new parents were academics and she had a sister who was three years older, a wayward soul in her previous life with lots to prove if she was eventually to move on to the good side. There was also a brother who was a new soul without any history.

They could see Amanda was deep in thought but none dared interrupt her.

'If he asks,' said Raphael, 'we don't lie or hide the truth; but if he doesn't, we send them on. He'll find out eventually then all will become clear.'

4

Raphael had given her the news that she wasn't allowed to help her brothers with the trouble that was to come. It had taken Claire some time to process and come to terms with this information and she recalled the conversation. 'But if I can't help my own family, what hope is there for me?'

'We are here for the greater good, Claire. For the love of mankind and not simply to help those with whom we have special bonds. I'm not saying it's easy but it is right, and if you are to fulfil your destiny and progress as an angel, you have to make some hard choices.'

'And what if I decide to go against the advice? That the love for my brothers outweighs the greater good?'

'Then you're not the angel any of us thought you were and there'll be consequences. We've all been through this, Claire, to get to where we are now. I know how you feel.'

Keeping himself perfectly still and calm and maintaining a surface smile, Raphael put a hand on her leg underneath the table in the hope it would calm her.

Claire knew she'd had plenty of time to come to terms with the fact that she couldn't help her family on this occasion but felt better having given her brothers a message. It was now up to them how they dealt with it.

She opened her mouth to ask who was to give Ron and Sandy the news and take them to the entrance - not having been selected for this job previously, she was excited, hoping it was her turn but was beaten to the punch.

'Raphael,' said his mother. 'You will give them the news and see them to the entrance.' Then she saw the look on Claire's face and felt guilty for winding her up. Her son's soul mate was a talented junior angel but still too impatient, so even though it was very unangelic of her, Amanda occasionally liked to remind Claire who was boss.

Claire tensed. *Surely she wouldn't send Raphael alone without giving her the opportunity to say farewell to Ron?* She remembered how they'd arrived in Cherussola together, and the day she was told a mistake had been made and she'd been taken before her time. It all seemed so long ago now, and hers wasn't the only life that had changed. She looked at Raphael. Claire thought she'd loved Jay, her fiancée, before death. But the feelings she had for Raphael were ten thousand times deeper than those she'd felt for Jay. She smiled and, without looking at her, he gave her leg a squeeze in acknowledgement. She felt a deep rush of love. *I'll be grateful that Ron and Sandy are going to be happy for eternity,* she thought, *and happy that my angel is the one selected to take them on the journey.*

As Claire tried desperately to convince herself that she would be gracious about not going, Amanda's voice interrupted her thoughts. 'Are you still with us, my dear?'

Claire returned to the present with a jolt. Amanda hadn't called her *my dear* before and it made her feel two hundred years old.

'You have two challenges. This is your first.'

'Why is this a challenge and what's the second?' she asked, as Amanda knew she would.

'You have to complete the first to my satisfaction, before the second will be revealed. All in good time,' said the senior angel who Claire thought of as a heavenly mother-in-law, albeit a mother-in-law who had the ability to wind her up.

Claire gave her wings a gentle wiggle and checked her feathers as she'd got into the habit of doing recently, to help her curb her natural curiosity and impatience. She still needed to prove to them all that she could be trusted and not always act on impulse. 'As you wish,' she said, resisting the urge to ask further questions and attempting to look as angelic as possible.

Amanda suppressed a smile. 'Claire, you will, of course, accompany Raphael. I trust you to answer any of Ron's questions truthfully and cleverly. Do you think you're up to the task?'

'Yes, Amanda. Oh, yes.' She did an internal jig and tried to look as if it was a normal meeting with an everyday task.

'Thank you for trusting me,' she added. Claire knew it sounded sycophantic but meant every word.

'Leave now and report back to me when the mission and your first challenge is over.'

Dismissed, they got up from the table and left the chambers.

Chapter 2 – The Netherlands, Years Earlier

It was Saturday and market day in Archilen, a Dutch border town between Germany and Holland. The area was buzzing with a mix of people; Germans, some Brits from the nearby military bases, and lots of locals. Marc and Kat Van Toulen were two of the latter, but they hardly noticed the crowds around them.

'Are you going to be in a huff all day?' Marc asked his wife.

'Well, you did say you'd be home in time for dinner, and yet again I had to throw it away. I wouldn't mind if you just did what you said…'

'None of the other guys get this sort of hassle and I'm fed up with it. You know there was a match on so what do you expect?'

'I expect you to do what you say you're going to do! Just for once would be nice.'

A few people looked their way as Kat raised her voice but they soon went back to their own business.

'Don't you ever talk to me like that in public.' Marc squeezed her upper arm tightly, to make his point.

'Ow, you're hurting me!'

He dropped his hand, then stepped in front of her so she was forced to stop walking, and leaned his face down into his wife's. 'You're turning into a proper nag. It's only once a week, for God's sake, and it's not like we've got kids you need me to help you with or anything.'

'Oh, that old chestnut. And whose fault is it that we haven't got kids? Eh, Marc? Answer me that?'

'Well there's nothing wrong with me. You need to go back to that doctor and get him to check again,' Marc retorted, his face red from trying to keep his voice down and hold his temper in public. Deciding it was too difficult, he turned around and started to walk away.

He was a tall man with a long stride, so Kat had to rush to catch up with him. She couldn't believe they were having this conversation while walking down the high street.

'There's no reason I can't have children,' she said quietly, pulling at his arm so he stopped walking and faced her directly again. 'You're in total denial about this. How many times do I have to ask you to go get yourself checked? If there's anything wrong, Marc, there's a good chance you can have treatment and they can sort it. And if not, there's always other ways. We could have IVF or even…'

'You're obsessed with this, Kat. Totally obsessed.'

'*I'm* obsessed!' Kat was trying her best to keep her cool, but he was driving her nuts. 'You raised the subject in the middle of the flaming town centre for goodness sake, and you call *me* obsessed?'

'You need to get a life, Kat, so you have something else to think about.'

'So, I need to get a life, do I?' Kat's face hardened. She turned on her heel and started to walk away.

'Where are you going?'

She turned and strode back towards him. 'I'm going to the Market Inn to meet Jessica and a few of my other friends. Or, I'm getting a life as you might care to think of it.'

'Good.' Marc felt the rage starting and he clenched and unclenched his fists trying to control his reaction. 'I hope you'll be in a better mood by the time

9

you get home...' He spat the words. 'If not, don't bother coming back.'

Now it was his turn to walk away. Kat had been watching him for a few seconds before he turned around. 'I'll get a takeaway,' he called, as if something to eat was the most important issue they had to deal with.

Kat shook her head, trying to get over the ridiculousness of her husband's last comment. Then she thought about the whole argument. She had expected him to apologise or to ask her not to go so they could spend some time together. But to say *'don't bother coming back'?* And then saying he'd get a flaming takeaway! Useless man, thinking of his stomach at a time like this. Did that mean he wanted a divorce? How could he? He wouldn't manage on his own - she did everything at home and he couldn't even cook a simple meal for himself. Furious, she stomped towards the pub, still determined to have a drink even though she'd made up the story about meeting her friends. By the time she got there, her mind was working overtime. She'd wondered for a while whether Marc still loved her, and, even if he was fertile, they probably didn't make love enough to conceive. Perhaps it was time for both of them to move on; after all, what was the point in being together if they constantly made each other unhappy.

She touched her arm where he had squeezed it. That had been cruel and it still hurt. He'd hurt her a few other times too. She put those to the back of her mind as she struggled to remember the last time they'd had fun or laughed together – it was a long time ago. They'd been married for eight years and she'd put up with his selfish behaviour for so long because she thought she loved him. But did she really?

As she entered the pub and took a seat in the nearest empty booth, Kat thought about her own parents; the way her mother always looked disappointed and her father could never do anything to make her happy. She would rather her and Marc split up than end up hating each other. Her father was a gentle giant and allowed her mother to walk all over him. Kat wondered if it was because of his heart condition that he seemed willing to do anything for what he considered an easy life.

'Penny for them?' The barman slid into the booth opposite Kat and smiled.

'Nothing interesting I'm afraid.'

'Well, I can see you're unhappy so I'm here if you need to chat. A problem shared and all of that. The name's Finn, by the way.'

He was younger than her and had what she could only describe as come-to-bed eyes. The guy was obviously used to getting his own way with the ladies, but she wasn't interested. 'You're all right, but thanks for the offer,' Kat said, deciding not to tell him her name in case he took it as encouragement. 'Can I get a vodka tonic please?'

'Coming right up,' he said. 'What did you say your name was?'

'I didn't. Just the drink please,' she replied, knowing she was being rude. But it did the trick and Finn disappeared, returning with her drink a few minutes later.

Kat took a book out of her bag but kept reading the same sentence over and over again. She gave up eventually and, instead, partook in one of her favourite hobbies; people watching. An older looking man approached, and she knew almost straight away that he was a complete chancer.

'And what's a beautiful lady like you doing on your own?' he asked, sitting himself on the seat opposite her. 'Mind if I join you?'

'Seeing as you ask, I do actually.'

11

The man ignored her. 'Like a drink? I can show you a real good time.'

'Good grief. Can't a woman have a drink on her own without being propositioned?'

'It's only a bit of fun, love,' he replied. 'And you can't blame a man for trying, especially with a lady as special as you.'

'I think I'm going to be sick,' she said, and he had the good grace to laugh but still didn't move.

Kat picked up her book.

'I'm Eric.'

She ignored him.

'This is where you tell me your name and…'

Kat sighed and put the book down. He was starting to annoy her now and she was about to tell him when another man appeared. Taller than Eric with fair hair and a kindly expression, he looked firstly at Eric and then at Kat. Her first instinct was that this man was trustworthy.

'Is he bothering you, love?'

'I would rather be on my own, yes.'

'She looked unhappy, so I was only trying to make her smile.'

'You heard the lady,' said the other man. 'No harm done if you come back to the bar, Eric, and leave the lady in peace.'

'And if I don't?'

The man laughed, and those kindly eyes twinkled. 'Well I'd hate to lose your business, Eric, but I think I could live with it.'

Now it was Eric's turn to chuckle. 'If you change your mind,' he said to Kat as he stood up. 'I'll be back in a flash.'

She shook her head and rolled her eyes. 'Thanks,' she said to the other man as Eric made his way back to the bar.

'Sorry about that,' he said. 'We have a good mix of people coming in here and sometimes Eric's like a kid in a sweetie shop. I've threatened to ban him before but despite his cockiness, I think he's lonely.'

'I see. He's on his own then?'

'Yeah. He did the dirty on his wife and she left him. He was with someone else for a while but kept trying to chat up other women, so she disappeared, too. It's almost as if he can't help himself. I don't know what's wrong with the man.'

'It takes all sorts,' said Kat.

'It certainly does. I'm Frank, and I'm the owner of this place.' He swung his arm around to show her his domain. 'Can I get you a drink by way of apology for my staff and for Eric being a nuisance?'

'That's really kind of you, but there's no need, honestly.'

'Okay, but can I make a suggestion?'

Kat nodded.

'If you enjoy people watching and don't want to be disturbed, I have a much better booth for you where you can see people coming and going but they're less likely to notice you.'

'Sounds perfect,' said Kat. As she picked up her bag and book, Frank picked up her drink and she followed him to a booth that looked private but had a good view of the bar. *Where I can wallow in my own misery without anyone noticing*, she thought.

Feeling deflated, Kat finished her drink shortly after and left. She needed to sort out their problems whatever the outcome.

She was surprised to find that Marc wasn't home and decided to make a sandwich instead of waiting for a take-away, and watch some TV for a few hours. There was a new show where ordinary members of the public sang before a panel of famous people who voted to either to give them a chance and put them

13

through to the next round, or to shatter their dreams and send them back home. A woman who looked a similar age to Kat had a lovely voice but the panel didn't give her a chance and Kat watched as the woman left the stage trying to hold back her tears. Behind the stage the woman ran to a man who, the narrator explained, was her father. When her father hugged her, the floodgates opened. Something resonated and Kat burst into tears, realising that her own life wasn't working out as planned, and her own hopes and dreams were coming to nothing.

She wasn't yet aware that those dreams would soon turn to nightmares.

She took herself off to bed and cried herself to sleep. Much later, Marc banging around downstairs woke her and she waited for him to come to bed. She waited for a long time. Eventually realising he wasn't coming up to bed, she gave up and, after tossing and turning for a while, drifted off into a restless sleep. Despite feeling like crap when she got up on Sunday morning, she decided to go easy on him and make them a breakfast treat. Marc was flat out on the sofa, so she prepared the coffee and had a few slurps before starting on the breakfast. The strong coffee aroma filled the kitchen and as the caffeine hit her bloodstream, Kat started to feel more human, but knew she wouldn't feel better until Marc agreed to discuss their problems. In an attempt to put those thoughts on hold, she took a bowl out of the cupboard and prepared the egg and milk to dip the bread in, and after doing so, added the cinnamon. She heard Marc coughing as she put the bread in the pan. Kat poured him a coffee and took it over to him.

'Good morning,' she said as she put down the mug and watched him sit up. 'How are you today?'

'Shit, thanks to you,' he replied. He picked up the mug and took a swig of coffee.

Kat felt the hairs on the back of her neck stand on end, like a dog's hackles rising before a fight. 'Thanks to me? You were the one who decided to go and get wrecked instead of talking like a proper, well-adjusted adult. I don't know what's wrong with you Marc but…'

'Don't know what's wrong with me? Let me tell you then, Kat. You nag me as soon as I wake up; you can't give me a child…' He looked at her, shaking his head. '…You're basically a fucking nightmare and we're over.' He pushed himself up from the sofa and headed for the bathroom door.

'I'm a nightmare and we're over? What about…' Kat's words were drowned out by the door slamming behind him and she ran to the lounge and flung herself on the sofa, sobbing her heart out. She knew they had problems but despite her thoughts of the previous afternoon had never really imagined that their marriage was over. She thought she loved Marc, but her emotions were all over the place and now, like yesterday, she wasn't sure how she felt.

The noise from the smoke detector forced her to move and Kat ran to the kitchen, turned off the pan and opened the window and back door. Next, she opened the windows in the lounge and the noise from the detector stopped a few seconds later. *What do I do now?* she wondered. Was there any point in speaking to him? She thought she knew her husband well, but the man who'd spoken to her this morning was a stranger, a stranger who no longer wanted to be with her. He'd left his phone on the side table next to the sofa when he'd returned the night before and it bleeped. Kat knew she shouldn't, but picked it up anyway. *Morning, handsome,* she read. *Thanks for last night, can't wait to do it again. L x.*

'Who the hell…?' she said out loud as the earlier self-pity turned to anger. She stomped to the bathroom. Marc was in the shower, and she screamed over the sound of the running water.

'We have one argument and you find another woman? Who is she? Who is she...?'

Marc opened the shower door and watched as his wife threw his phone onto the tiled floor where it shattered apart.

'I didn't find another woman last night,' he said.

'But I've read the text she sent, you must have...'

'I've been seeing Lotte for a while, Kat. I'm sorry, I should have...'

'Sorry! You're sorry? I've been trying to work things out to save our marriage and all this time you've been screwing around with some tart named Lotte? How could you, Marc?'

'Because we're not working, and you never listen to me.' He calmly dried himself as he gave her the devastating news, as if they were having a normal conversation. 'And you can't give me a baby. There's something wrong with you, Kat, and...'

'I can't give you a baby? How many times do I have to tell you? I've had all the tests, Marc, you're in total denial. It's you who's firing blanks. But never mind that. If you loved me enough, you'd see the doctor and we could have...' Kat's voice trailed off, she knew their marriage was over and it was too late now, for a baby, or anything else for that matter. 'Get out,' she said.

'I'll work something out and move out when...'

'No. Get out of here now. I can't stand the sight of you!'

'But you can't throw me out of my own home. We both pay the rent and...'

'Pack your bags, Marc, and leave. Unless you want all your stuff to end up just like your phone.' Kat's look told him she wasn't messing so he dried and dressed hurriedly. Packing some of his gear, he did as ordered.

'I'm going because it's my decision and I want to be with a real woman,' he said, gripping her arms too tightly and staring down menacingly into her face. 'And when I come for the rest of my stuff, make sure you're not in. I don't want to see your pathetic, ugly face, ever again.'

Kat leaned against the wall shaking after he'd left, surprised at the cruelty of the words and the menace in his voice. Unsure whether she was frightened or heartbroken, at least she could wallow in her pain and misery now and wouldn't have to spend any more time looking at him.

Kat cried and cried. By the afternoon she was all cried out and phoned Jessica.

'I was just about to phone you,' her best friend told her. 'My mum's had a heart attack, we're leaving for Amsterdam now.'

'Is there anything I can do?'

'No, Kat. It's touch and go and I just need to get there as soon as I can.'

'Phone me if you need anything.'

'Will do.'

There was no way Kat was telling her best friend about her own problems when she had a life and death situation to deal with. She didn't want to discuss her life with any of her other friends; most of them were couples and friends of them both, but if she stayed at home any longer, she knew she'd go crazy. Her marriage was over, and it felt weird. She had to get out and think things through and get the anger that was eating away at her out of her system.

She took a quick shower and put on her running kit, then she pounded the streets and park for a good forty minutes, in an attempt to stop the devastating thoughts from running around and around in her head. She was shattered when she got home but didn't feel any better. Not wanting to be on her own, she showered again, did her hair and make-up in an attempt to make herself look presentable, then dressed and left the apartment. *Perhaps I should do exactly what Marc has,* she thought to herself as she headed for the Market Inn.

The first two vodkas went down hardly touching the sides, and by the time she ordered the third from the friendly barman, Kat was feeling very squiffy. 'Where's Frank today?' she asked.

'Off with his family,' Finn, the man who'd initially sat in the booth with her the day before replied. 'His wife's due to give birth any day now.'

'Ah,' said Kat, trying to hide her disappointment.

'I get off in an hour,' he said. 'Do you fancy some company?'

'Why not.' She leaned on the bar towards him, looking into his come-to-bed eyes and gave him a suggestive smile, trying to replicate the one he gave her. 'Why not indeed.'

When she woke up the following morning in Finn's bed, Kat had a banging headache. Other than that, she had no regrets and, without worrying or even thinking about Marc, found she felt better than she had in ages. She sat up in bed and looked at the man she'd had wild, rampant, sex with. He was still sleeping but had thrown the quilt off the top of his body. She looked at that body for the first time, without the haze of alcohol, then moved her eyes up to his face. He was, perhaps, in his early to mid-twenties – maybe five or six years younger than Kat. She didn't usually like hairy men but it obviously hadn't bothered her enough to stop her as she vaguely remembered tickling his chest the night before. *Should I be ashamed of my behaviour? After all, I'm still a married woman.* Kat smiled to herself. For the first time in ages someone had enjoyed her company, listened to her (as far as she could remember), and desired her. But what now? She had the rest of her life to live without Marc and…

'Hello, beautiful.' Finn, the handsome stranger was awake.

'Good morning.'

It was his turn to smile and he held out his arms towards her as he did so. Kat didn't hesitate. She turned fully towards him and kissed him on the lips. It wasn't long before he was on top of her again and all her problems were put back in the box for later.

When she woke, sometime later, Kat knew it was time to go. She kissed her new lover and told him.

'Thanks, baby. Let's do this again sometime.'

She realised it was a good job she hadn't planned on this being anything other than a one-night stand and it had made her feel wanted. As she put the key into the apartment door, reality hit and she realised that although the previous night had eased her wounds, it would take her a while to get over her marriage. You couldn't love someone for so long and forget about them overnight – even if they had treated you like muck.

Life continued. Jessica called on the Tuesday, to inform Kat she would be remaining in Amsterdam to look after her mother when she left hospital. Jessica's husband was in the finance business and though she worked in a large department store, they didn't need her wages to survive.

'K and M's said there's always vacancies in the fashion or food department,' she told Kat, 'so I'll be able to go back to work whenever I want. I'm just very worried about Mum, Kat, and I want to be here for her. Lucas is supporting my decision and he's going to join me at the weekends.'

Kat was so glad her best friend had the support of the man she loved. Their marriage was rock solid, or seemed to be, she corrected herself. Rock solid is what she'd thought she and Marc were, and look what had happened to them.

'I haven't even asked how you are?'

'I'm fine, same old, same old.'

'You don't sound it, Kat. You seem a bit down. Are you sure everything's all right?'

My husband has been seeing someone else for God knows how long, my marriage is over, and I had a one-night stand with a guy years younger than me, but other than that I'm fine.

Kat knew Jess would worry if she told her the truth, but she also knew that she'd have to tell her something.

'I'm a bit tired. I had another argument with Marc, and he still refuses to get checked out. We seem to be at an impasse and we're both fed up.'

'I see. What are you going to do?'

'I honestly don't know, Jess, but I'll let you know as soon as I do.'

'Well I'm here to talk if you need me, just remember that.'

Kat said she would, and they hung up shortly after. She hated lying to her friend but justified it by deciding she'd tell her everything when she came home. In the meantime, she had to engage the services of a lawyer and start divorce proceedings. She made a call and an appointment was arranged for the following week.

*****

Marc soon realised he'd made a mistake. Having a mistress had been great fun and Lotte loved a good time. What she didn't enjoy was nights in, in front of the television, domestic chores, or anything she considered boring.

'I didn't ask you to leave your wife,' she said.

20

'But I thought we loved each other and wanted to make a home together?'

'No, Marc. That's what you wanted. I only went along with it because I thought you were a typical man who would never leave his wife. Turns out I was wrong. It was fun when it lasted but…'

'No need to say anymore, Lotte. I get it. I'll sleep on the sofa tonight and be out of your hair tomorrow.'

Lotte laughed. 'No need for that, darling.' When she saw the look of hope in his eyes, she corrected herself. 'I mean there's no need to sleep on the sofa. Why don't we make our last night together one to remember? Get yourself a drink while I get ready.'

Lotte disappeared into the bedroom while Marc got a beer out of the fridge and contemplated his future. Less than twenty minutes later she walked into the living room wearing a silk mini dressing gown, tied at the waist. She leaned over to nuzzle Marc's ear, before nibbling his upper lip. When she stood up again, he could see part of her suspenders, holding up a stocking. She slowly untied the belt at her waist, and he gasped as he always did when she revealed the curves of her magnificent body. Lotte put a foot on the couch and Marc ran his fingers from her ankle to her thighs, then attempted to undo the suspender.

'Patience,' she said, laughing. She moved away and started unlacing the front of her basque.

All thoughts of Marc's long-term future disappeared as he was lost in the moment.

'Follow me,' said Lotte, and he complied, like an enthusiastic little puppy.

It was the best night of his life, but he was still glad to leave the following day. He packed hastily after taking a shower and having a quick breakfast.

21

'If you're ever in need of some fun, you know where I am,' she said as she closed the door behind him, not bothering to ask what his plans were for the future.

Marc knew Kat would take him back, even if it took a while to convince her. He went to the office as usual, deciding to go to the apartment to talk to her after work. Kat worked shifts at the hospital, so he had to call her first to check she was going to be home.

'Can we talk when I finish work today?'

'I have nothing to say to you,' Kat replied. 'You can communicate through my lawyer.'

'Don't be like that, Kat. I still have some stuff in the apartment I need to sort, so when's a good time to come?'

She sighed, knowing he was right but determined not to be there. 'You can collect your stuff at any time. You still have keys. I don't need to be there for that. Leave the keys on the hook when you've finished and close the door on your way out. Now I have to get back to work.'

The line went dead and Marc looked at his new phone in disbelief. *She has to realise she's been punching above her weight all the time we've been together, surely?* he thought, unwilling to accept that she might be serious about the split and wouldn't even talk to him, even though she had no idea what he wanted to discuss. He drove to a local deli and, not knowing how long he'd have to wait, bought a coffee and some sandwiches. Parking his car outside the apartment, he let himself in and ate the sandwich while he settled in to wait until she returned home.

After less than an hour he heard the key in the door.

'Hello, Kat.' Marc gave her his best smile. 'I've missed you.'

'What the hell are you doing here?'

22

'I thought we could talk and…'

'We have nothing to talk about. You deceived me and made my life a misery. We're finished.'

'I made a mistake, Kat, I'll grant you that. But we had problems and I turned to someone else for help. It's over now and we can get our marriage back on track.'

Kat looked at the man she'd thought she'd known inside out and realised that she didn't know him at all. 'I was devastated when you left Marc…'

That's exactly what I want to hear, he thought, until she continued.

'…but it didn't take long for me to realise that the only person important in your life is you…'

'That's not true, I…'

'Let me finish! I've had plenty of time to think and, looking back through the years, I've put up with too much selfish behaviour from you. As well as being selfish, you're controlling, unkind, and useless around the apartment. You've also taken my good nature for granted and are totally in denial about not being able to father a child. Our marriage is over!'

Marc closed his eyes for a second, struggling to keep his temper in check. Kat could see his fists clenching and unclenching – a sure sign of danger – so decided not to add her opinion about his performance in the bedroom; she'd said enough for the time being.

'I think you'd better just get your stuff and go.'

'But this is my apartment too, and I need…' He stopped himself from saying he needed somewhere to stay, but he was too late, she'd guessed the rest of the sentence. Her earlier resolve about not winding him up further crumbled.

'So that didn't last very long did it? Has she decided she doesn't want to live with you either? Why is that, Marc? Maybe you couldn't perform the way she wanted you to, eh?' said Kat, then laughed derisively to rub it in.

The punch seemed to come out of nowhere and knocked her sideways onto the floor. She screamed, staring up at the man she'd once loved. Putting her hands to the floor, she pushed herself to her feet slowly and carefully. She could feel her eye closing and put a hand to her cheek, which was already swelling. Looking at the man in front of her, she felt frightened, but tried not to show it. 'Get out…,'

'Kat, I'm sorry, I didn't mean to…'

'…Now, before I phone the police.' She picked up her phone and moved towards the bedroom door, knowing she could lock herself in safely if the situation became more serious.

Marc hesitated and she wondered what he was going to do. Then the temper seemed to leave him just as quickly as it arrived. 'Okay, I'm going. Take a look in the mirror, Kat. You're punching well above your weight and know you'll never meet anyone as good as me. This isn't over by a long chalk. I'll be in touch when you've come to your senses.'

'What do I have to do to get through to you, Marc?' she called after him, but he'd already left.

Kat tossed and turned that night, tormented both by the pain in her cheek and Marc's words. Looking as dreadful as she felt the following morning, she went straight to the hospital and the x-ray confirmed her cheek bone had a slight fracture, but there was no long-term damage.

'You're lucky he didn't break your nose,' the doctor said, once she'd told him what had happened. 'Have you reported him to the police?'

'It was a one-off,' she replied, 'and my lawyer is going to deal with him, so I don't have to. I'll never speak to him again.'

The doctor was satisfied that Kat would make a complete recovery and they left it at that.

But she was wrong. He kept calling her.

'You know you can't live without me.'

She hung up.

'Why would you do this after all I've done for you?'

'You love me really. You just want to hurt me for having an affair.'

The first few times she tried reasoning with him. 'Neither of us were happy together, Marc, that's why you had an affair. Let's just let our lawyers deal with it. It'll be easier for the both of us and I haven't reported that incident to the police, but if you continue to harass me…' She left the last words unspoken, but Marc had turned into a person Kat no longer knew. Nothing she said seemed to stop his growing obsession with her and she started to worry. She was feeling out of sorts and stuffing her face with cakes, chocolates and anything sweet she could get her hands on. Kat knew her weight gain was due to her unhealthy diet, and when she missed her first period she put it down to stress.

On the way home from work on the evening she realised she'd skipped her second period, Kat had the eerie feeling she was being watched. Marc's behaviour was making her feel increasingly nervous and she gave herself a mental shake, trying to put him out of her mind. *I've more important things to deal with*, she told herself as she entered the pharmacy and bought a pregnancy test.

Back at home, she sat on the edge of the bath already knowing what the result would be.

'I'm going to be a mum!' she said out loud, as she watched the second blue line appear on the stick. Then she burst into tears. When she'd pulled herself together, Kat made a cup of tea and sat down to think.

She hadn't seen Finn, the baby's father, since their one-night stand, and as much as she'd enjoyed herself, it wasn't her style and she certainly didn't want a relationship with him. Kat assumed that Finn would feel the same, but the guy deserved to know he was going to be a father. She'd tell him once she'd wrapped her own head around the idea.

And what about Marc? If his recent behaviour was anything to go by, he would go off on one. The health and welfare of her baby was paramount, so she decided not to tell him. If she was unfortunate enough to bump into him during the latter stages of pregnancy, Kat was convinced that his behaviour would have changed by then and he would have moved on. She needed someone to talk to and this was an emergency. She rang the number Jess had given her.

'Hello! How are you and how's your mum?'

Jess was in tears. 'I've just had a call from the hospital, Kat. They don't think Mum's going to last the night.'

'But I thought she was getting better?'

'She was, but now she has sepsis and the antibiotics aren't working. Kat, I have to go.'

'I'm so sorry, Jess. I'll take time off work and come to Amsterdam…'

'I'll probably need you more when I come home,' Jess replied. 'I'll phone you as soon as I have some news.'

'Take care, Jess.' They hung up and Kat cried again. Her emotions were all over the place and the one friend with whom she shared the intimate details of her life had her own problems. Kat wondered briefly whether she should talk to her parents. She ruled the idea out almost as soon as it entered her head. One of the reasons Kat and Marc had married eight years ago instead of living together first, was because her parents, *my mother,* Kat corrected herself, were dead against anyone living under the same roof out of wedlock. Unlike most Dutch people, her mother was a staunch Catholic and insisted on doing things by the book. Her father went along with whatever her mother wanted, and if they knew that the baby wasn't Marc's, her mother would be less than happy. In fact, thought Kat, she would be extremely angry and would probably berate Kat for her behaviour for years to come. This was something else to consider and she didn't know how her parents would feel about her baby when he or she was born.

'You poor little thing,' she said, looking down and rubbing her belly. 'All these problems and you're still just a tiny human. But I love you already and even if it's just you and me, kid, we'll be all right.'

*****

Jess phoned the following day. 'She's dead, Kat. I held her hand as she passed…' The floodgates opened, and Kat could do nothing but listen until they subsided.

'I'm so sorry, Jess. I know it doesn't make it any easier, but at least your mum is at peace, and she's not suffering anymore.'

'I know. But that doesn't stop it hurting like hell. Lucas has been great and he's making all of the funeral arrangements. I don't know what I'd do without him.'

'I'm so glad he's there to support you,' said Kat, 'I can come too if…'

'We're going to sort out her belongings,' Jess said. There was silence while she gulped back some more tears, trying to compose herself. 'That'll keep me busy until the funeral next week and we'll come home the following day. Thanks for the offer, Kat, but maybe when I get back you can take a few days off and we can spend some time together? I've missed you and…'

27

'Of course, Jess. I'll do that. I've missed you too.' Now it was Kat's turn to cry.

'Are you okay?'

Kat gave an embarrassed laugh. 'Of course. I just feel for you that's all.'

After crying together for a few minutes, they finished the call. There was nothing Kat could do now to help her friend. She felt selfish thinking about their get together when Jess returned, knowing that she'd be able to talk about everything at long last. It couldn't come soon enough for Kat. Before that, it was time to speak to the baby's father.

Kat went home to change after work the following day. Dressed in jeans and baggy top, she tried to hide the fact that her breasts were bigger and that she'd put on a bit of weight. She took a deep breath, walked into the Market Inn and approached the bar. A quick check showed that Finn wasn't behind the bar and neither was Frank.

'Soda water please.' She smiled at the young woman behind the bar, '...with a slice of lime but no ice. Is Finn about?' she asked.

The barmaid put Kat's drink on the bar. 'Finn? I don't know anyone named Finn, but I've only been here for a week.'

'Is Frank about?'

'Yeah, he's in the back doing some paperwork.'

'Could you get him for me please?'

'He said he doesn't want to be disturbed, and I don't want to get into trouble.'

'Pretty please,' said Kat. 'I really need to speak to him.'

The girl frowned but said okay and disappeared through to the back. Frank appeared a few minutes later.

'Hello again, Kat,' he said. 'Nice to see you.'

'And you,' she replied. 'How's your wife?'

'Fine thanks. We're now the proud parents of Angelina, born two weeks ago-and she's turned our world upside down!' He was beaming and his smile was infectious.

'Congratulations! I'm so happy for you and your family. It must be wonderful.'

'It is, and look,' he said, taking his wallet out of his pocket and producing a photograph.

Kat looked at the photo of Frank's wife and their baby girl, whose head was covered in a mop of blonde hair.

She oohed and aahed over the photograph before saying, 'They're both gorgeous.'

'I know. I'm a very lucky man. Now what can I do for you?'

The barmaid was leaning forward with her elbows on the bar, her hands cupping her chin, and listening quite openly.

Kat walked out of her hearing distance and Frank followed. 'I need to speak to Finn,' she said. 'Can you tell me when he's next on shift?'

'Not you too!' Frank said, his smile disappearing.

'Pardon?'

'You're the third woman in this week asking for Finn. He left two weeks ago, the day after I paid him, and I haven't seen hide nor hair of him since.'

'So, I take it he didn't leave a forwarding address?'

'No, nothing.'

'Can you tell me his last name?'

'His full name is Finn Visser; well, that's the name he gave me anyway. But I shouldn't bother trying to find him, Kat.' Seeing her expression, he elaborated. 'One of the other women came back in. She went onto the World Wide Web to try to find him. You know how popular the name Visser is, but she couldn't find

29

anyone matching Finn's description from Amsterdam, and she's hired a detective to help her.'

'Really? She must be desperate to find him. But what about his social insurance wouldn't they...'

'I paid him cash in hand, and I really wouldn't want...'

'Of course. I don't intend to pursue this anyway,' she said, rubbing her belly subconsciously.

'Oh, you're not...'

Kat realised she'd given the game away before he finished his sentence. 'I certainly am. I'm not usually one for one-night stands but my husband and I had problems. We've since separated and...'

'You don't have to justify yourself to me, Kat.'

'I know, but let's just say my behaviour was out of character.' She smiled. 'I'm overjoyed at the prospect of having a baby and don't need a wayward father to screw up my child's life.'

'You know it's not going to be easy, bringing up a child on your own, don't you?'

'I'll soon find out.' She gave a wry smile. 'Thanks for the information, Frank, and congratulations again. You're a lucky man.'

'I am,' he said, and smiled again. 'Take care, Kat, and if you need to talk, you know where I am.'

She left the bar feeling happy that she'd done her best to speak to the baby's father, and happy in the knowledge that she couldn't contact him.

As she walked down the High Street, Kat had the strange feeling yet again that she was being watched. She looked around but didn't see anything or anyone out of the ordinary. Shrugging, she put it down to everything that had happened within the last few months; or maybe it was a protective instinct to the baby she was carrying? Either way, she brushed it off, and would later come to regret the fact that she hadn't trusted her gut.

*****

Jess was home! It seemed like an age since they'd seen each other and so much had happened in the five months since she'd left that Kat wasn't sure where to start. They hugged as soon as Jess answered the door, both women crying with sadness for Jess's loss, and with the joy of their reunion. Jess didn't know yet that Kat's tears were for many other reasons.

'I'm so sorry for your loss, Jess. Your mum was a lovely woman and I know how close you were.'

'I know. Saying goodbye at her funeral was the hardest thing I've ever done. But I keep consoling myself with the fact that she's no longer in pain and she wouldn't have made a complete recovery from the sepsis. I'll always miss her but...'

'She's in a better place now, eh?' Kat said, taking Jess's hand in hers.

'Yeah, I guess. But it doesn't make it any easier. Not yet anyway.'

'I'm sorry.'

'What about you, Kat. I know something's not right and I guess you felt I had enough going on without you adding to my problems?'

Kat nodded sadly.

'Well I'm home now. Shall I open a bottle of wine and you can tell me all about it.'

'I'll just have a glass of water thanks.'

'I knew it! You're pregnant, aren't you?'

'Yup.'

'But I thought that you and Marc... I mean I got the impression that you two weren't getting on that well and...'

'You're right, Jess, we've split up and we're going to get a divorce. He was having an affair.'

'What! So you're pregnant and he's having an affair? What a total bastard! You wait until I see him, I'll certainly give him a piece of my mind!'

31

Kat laughed and Jess stopped talking.

'What's the joke? Am I missing something here?'

It's great to have her back, thought Kat, knowing she could tell her friend anything and everything and she would still love her, despite her weaknesses or mistakes. 'I found out about Marc's affair before I got pregnant, Jess, and he's not the father.'

'What the…?'

'You're right that our marriage has been on the rocks for a while. I kept trying to get things back on track and he was in denial that we couldn't have children. You know I had all the tests? Well he refused point blank and I thought that was driving a wedge between us. But looking back, there was a lot of other stuff that I ignored for most of the time we were together.'

Jess nodded occasionally as she listened to Kat and made encouraging noises for her to continue.

'Like when he expects me to do everything at home just because I'm a woman, and he stays out until whatever time he wants whenever he feels like it. But on the rare occasions I've been out with you and the other girls and it's been a late one, he's lost his temper the following day and hasn't spoken to me for days after. He also told me that I was punching above my weight and lucky to have him.' She decided not to tell her that he'd fractured her cheek bone, given her a black eye, and scared her at times; all this other information was enough for Jess to get her head around.

'He told you that? Well he had that the wrong way around so he's stupid as well as being a selfish prick!'

Kat laughed. 'Thanks, Jess. I feel better already.'

'So, tell me about the father. When do I get to meet him? Bring him to dinner one night with me and Lucas and we can give him the once over.'

'Like you did with Marc?' asked Kat, smiling cynically. As a couple, they had dined together once with Jess and her husband, Lucas, at their home and had never been invited back. It was no secret that both Jess and her husband disliked Marc.

Jess seemed to read her mind. 'You're right. It's no secret how I feel about Marc, Kat. He's a waste of space and I'm glad you're no longer together. Does he know about the baby and your new bloke?'

'No, and there isn't a new bloke.'

'But I…'

'It was a much needed one-night stand and when I went to his workplace to tell him about the baby, he'd left without a trace.'

'Oh, for the love of…'

'It's all right, Jess. I'm fine. Honestly I am. Finn wasn't the type of man I'd have a long-term relationship with anyway and I had no intention of jumping out of the frying pan and into the fire. I'm determined to do this on my own and my main worry now is Marc finding out about it. He came to see me and wanted us to get back together.' Kat changed her mind and decided to tell Jess everything. The floodgates were open, and it was as if she couldn't stop now. 'When I told him to get lost, he punched me in the face and I had to threaten to call the police. He left eventually but told me it's not the end and ever since then, I've felt like I've been walking on eggshells.'

'Oh, Kat! You had all this going on while I was away, and I bet you didn't talk to anyone else about it?'

'Of course not. Who else could I trust to keep this to themselves and not to judge me?' Feeling sorry for herself, Kat started crying again and Jess enveloped her in a warm hug. She lifted her head once the tears

33

had subsided. 'It's so great to have you back, Jess. I know it's selfish after everything you've been through, but it's been hard for me at times and I've missed not having you to talk to.'

'Well I'm back now and here whenever you need me. Move in with us for a while and I'll look after you.'

'That's really kind of you, Jess, but I need my own space and so do you two. We'd drive each other nuts!'

'Yeah, but it'd be fun too. How about we compromise, and you stay with us twice a week? I know I can look after you then.'

'That's lovely of you, Jess, and I may just take you up on that offer. I've missed you so much,' Kat said, bursting into tears again. 'I don't know what's wrong with me today, must be my flaming hormones or something.'

It's because I've been kind to her, thought Jess, knowing that Kat's mother seemed incapable of showing her even basic levels of consideration or support. She wished they'd had the same sort of relationship as she'd had with her own mother, and this made her miss her even more.

Kat left shortly after and as soon as she walked into her apartment, knew that someone had been in there. She noticed that a photograph was missing. She'd moved the photo of her and Marc from the side-table in the entrance hall and replaced it with one of her and Jess. Marc's keys were on the side-table where the photo used to be.

Why would he want a photo of me and Jess? She took a few deep breaths, as her doctor had advised her when she wanted to alleviate stress. She looked around the rest of the apartment, but nothing else was missing. Kat put the kettle on and made a mug of lemon tea. She sat down with the brew and put the TV on. A soap was playing, and she watched as the characters on the TV played out their lives, with much worse problems than hers. All the crying had drained her, and she decided that, as he'd left his keys, she would let the photograph go and wouldn't contact him. He should have received the letter from the lawyer by now so hopefully that, along with the keys, were signs that he'd finally come to terms with the fact their relationship was over, and he would leave her in peace to get on with the rest of the life.

Feeling optimistic, Kat went to bed and slept a dreamless sleep.

*****

Deciding it was time her parents knew the truth, she called them the next day to arrange a visit.

'Congratulations, my sweet, we're so happy for you aren't we, Bernhard?'

'Of course, my dear.' Her father put down his newspaper and agreed with her mother, as he always did. She remembered it being this way since she'd been a young child and wondered if he'd ever had a mind of his own.

'Boy or girl?'

'I'm having a girl, Mama,' Kat said, looking down and rubbing her stomach.

'Another girl in the family. Oh well. It's about time though,' her mother said. 'And where's Marc? You must both be over the moon.'

Kat's resolve left her. 'He's working, Mama, and said sorry he couldn't make it today.'

'Ah, good. He's out earning for his family. We understand, don't we, Bernhard?'

'Yes, dear.'

'You'll have to stop working so you'll need all the extra money he can earn. Good man.'

She was pleasantly surprised at her mother's reaction, having expected her to be annoyed that Marc wasn't with her.

'So, you are going to stop work? This baby needs its mama at home, not rushing around a hospital putting it in danger of God only knows what diseases and infections.'

Resisting the urge to remind her mother that she worked in an office in the hospital, she decided on the path of least resistance. 'Of course,' lied Kat. 'I'm finishing at the end of this month.'

'Good. And you don't need any of this nonsense about the father being there when you go in to give birth. Never happened in my day and doesn't need to happen now. I'll be there if I can, but if it's sudden and I can't make it in time, you'll have to go it alone. But we can be there shortly after the baby's born, can't we, Bernhard?'

'I'll try my best to get your mother there before the baby's born, my sweet. You don't want to be alone for such a traumatic event.'

'Traumatic event, pah!' said her mother. 'Of course we'll try to be there, Bernhard. But Kat can manage if we can't. When's the baby due?'

'October,' she lied, knowing her mother would have a go if she realised how far gone Kat was without telling her.

'You don't have to worry about this just yet, Kat,' her father said. 'But trust me that I'll move hell and high water to get to the hospital in time for our granddaughter's birth. I wouldn't miss this for the world.'

'Bernhard?'

Her mother looked at her father as if he'd grown horns, then she looked at Kat. Her father winked at her when her mother wasn't looking, and Kat felt a surge of love. She smiled at him and he got

36

up from his chair. They hugged as if her mother wasn't there and Kat had to hold back the tears, knowing that her mother would have a go if she started crying.

'I'll phone you,' he whispered, so quietly that she wondered if she'd imagined it. Then he added, '…when she's out.'

'No need for this silliness,' said her mother, taken aback at the affection they were showing each other.

They broke the hug and Kat made an excuse to use the bathroom. She was going to have secret conversations with her father and knew deep down that he'd be there to support her through this. A thought suddenly struck her that her father was in the same situation she had been in with Marc, and Kat wondered why he'd put up with her mother's controlling behaviour for so many years.

Back at work the following day, Kat spoke to the HR department and told them she intended to remain at her desk job until the end of July – a few weeks before her daughter's due date of mid-August.

*****

The routine during the next few weeks was work, home, catch up with Jess, then sleep. Besides for a few incidents of items seemingly going missing from the apartment, all was well. The relationship with her father was better than it had ever been, and Kat loved the weekly Wednesday evening call from him, when her mother was at her knitting circle. It was like her father had another side to him that she hadn't seen before and she loved him more than ever.

One Thursday evening she packed her bag ready to go to Jess. Lucas had planned a golf weekend away with friends, so Kat was going straight there after work. They'd planned a lazy weekend, lounging about and watching chic flicks, so she'd bought herself new pyjamas and a light summer dressing gown. She'd packed the PJs the previous night, but the dressing gown was missing. Kat recalled putting it on the hook on the back of the bedroom door after trying it on the night before. She wracked her brains and knew this was nothing to do with her hormones.

She phoned Jess. 'Marc's been here, I'm certain!'

'Okay. Take a deep breath and tell me what's happened. Has he hurt you?'

'No, Jess, nothing like that.' She did as her friend had advised and inhaled deeply. Jess waited patiently. 'I bought a new dressing gown and I'm one hundred percent certain I put it on the back of the door last night. It's not there now.'

'You're sure about this, Kat? I know some women have mummy brain when they're pregnant and can forget things…'

'I wish it was that but I'm absolutely positive. I'm frightened, Jess.'

'Okay, I'll get Lucas to phone an emergency locksmith and I'll be over as soon as I can.'

Lucas pointed to his watch and gave his wife an impatient look. Jess shrugged her shoulders.

'No need to come over, Jess, but you're right about changing the locks. If I can get that done tonight, I'll be fine.'

'You're sure?'

'Yeah, I'm sure.'

'Okay. We'll let you know the name of the locksmith and what time to expect him,' Jess said, and her husband gave her a thumbs up before digging out his address book and finding a number. 'Are you sure you'll be all right on your own tonight?'

'Absolutely. As long as I know Marc can't get in anymore, I'll be fine.'

'Give me a few minutes and I'll get back to you.'

Jess did as she promised and the locksmith was superb. By eight-thirty that evening, Kat's door had a new lock and she felt safe and secure in her home.

Her soon to be ex-husband watched the man with the toolbox return to his car. He knew he'd have to think of other ways to punish his wife for her behaviour.

*****

Kat returned to her apartment happy and relaxed on Sunday evening, and, after a quick check around, was pleased to see that nothing was missing. She unpacked and got her work clothes ready for the following day, then made a cup of lemon tea and sat down to watch TV. The phone rang ten minutes later.

'How could you, Kat?' her mother asked without first asking how she was or how her weekend had been.

'What, Mama? How could I what?' she asked, trying to process why her mother was so angry.

'Marc came to see us today. He's told us everything. You didn't tell him you were pregnant and that the baby isn't his!'

Oh shit! thought Kat, before reminding herself that he was the one who had had an affair and left their marriage. Her mother wouldn't see it like that though and Kat took a breath and prepared for the onslaught.

'You've acted like a trollop and brought shame on the family. You're a disgrace and I don't know how I'll be able to show my face in church again.'

'Don't be so harsh, my dear, and let Kat explain…' She heard her father in the background, trying to defend her.

'Shut up, Bernhard. I'm talking to Katherin.'

It was like a switch had clicked and Kat found courage from somewhere. 'Mama. Be quiet and listen to me for once.'

39

Her mother took the phone from her ear and looked at it as if it had just turned into a frog.

'Our marriage has been on the rocks for ages and I tried hard to paper over the cracks and to make it work. Unfortunately, Marc didn't try at all and decided to have an affair…'

'All men have…'

'Listen to me, Mama! I have no intention of living my life with a man who treats me like dirt and thinks it's acceptable to sleep with other women. I made a mistake, but it was after putting up with Marc's bad behaviour for years. You're right. Marc isn't the father of my baby, but you know what? I'm happier than I've been for ages and so looking forward to welcoming my baby girl to the world. And if you can't be happy for me, that's your problem.'

'You've wreaked havoc on this family and your only concern is your happiness? I don't know what I've done to deserve such a spoilt and selfish daughter, but I wash my hands of you, Katherin. You and your bastard child.'

'Mama!' But it was too late, the line was already dead. She banged the arm of the sofa, then cried tears of anger and frustration. Just as she was starting to form a loving relationship with her father, her mother had put paid to it and she was unsure when she'd speak to her father again. She was pleasantly surprised when she answered her ringing phone, some twenty minutes later.

'You've really done it this time.' It was her father's voice and Kat held her breath. 'She's only sent me out to get a bottle of sherry.' They giggled like a pair of five-year olds and when they finished, Kat's relief was palpable.

'I'm sorry, Pa, I didn't mean to bring shame on you and Mama. I couldn't stick it anymore and…'

40

'I'll let you into a little secret, Kat. I've never liked that husband of yours and I'm glad it's over. I'm excited about being a grandpapa and if I can't talk your mother around by the time my granddaughter is due to arrive, I'll come and visit on my own. I promise.'

'Papa, I…'

'It's all right, Kat. Everything's going to be all right.'

'It is now. And she's due to arrive in mid-August by the way.'

Her father gave a wry laugh. 'I thought you were a little bigger than expected. I have to go now, my sweet, but I'll call you every Wednesday as usual. I'm going to get one of those new- fangled mobile phones so you can call me at any time. 'Bye now.'

'Bye, Pa, and thanks.'

Kat hung up now feeling that everything would be all right. Then she remembered that Marc now knew she was pregnant. *Still, it'll save me having to tell him when we meet with our lawyers next week*, she thought, but despite her bravado and remembering when he'd punched her, she was still nervous about seeing him face to face.

The meeting with their lawyers was cancelled the day before it was due. 'He's agreed to sign the papers,' the legal secretary told her over the phone.

'So the divorce can proceed as planned?'

'That's right, yes.'

Kat was relieved that she didn't have to see him face to face and hoped he'd now leave her alone.

The opposite happened.

Saturday had come around again and she was meeting Jess for a proper catch up and lunch in town.

'How are you?' Kat asked.

Jess explained she missed her mother and was still struggling. 'I've heard people say that time's a great healer, but not for me. When I see something I think

41

she would like or want to tell her something I know she'd find amusing, I go to pick up the phone and then I remember. I know it's a cliché, Kat, but I'd do anything to have just one last conversation with her, to tell her how much she means to me and how she's shaped my life. I'd also ask her how I'm supposed to manage without her.' Jess fought back the tears and Kat took her friend's hand in her own.

'Oh, isn't that just so sweet,' said an angry voice from behind them. Kat didn't need to look to see who was the owner of that voice.

As the people at the other tables stopped talking, Jess looked at Kat and saw naked fear in her eyes.

'She doesn't want to be with you anymore, Marc,' she said in a quiet and reasoned voice. 'Why don't you leave her alone and move on with your own life?'

'This is between me and my wife,' he said, the tone of his voice now reasonable. 'And if you insist on visiting places when I'm already there, what do you expect me to do? Ignore the fact that my wife is having someone else's baby?'

There were gasps from some of the other tables and Marc tried to hide the satisfaction he felt.

'Because you had an affair and were a bastard to her for years!' said Jess, knowing that Kat wouldn't be happy to have her business shared in public, but she had an overwhelming need to defend her best friend. 'Now why don't you go back to your own table and leave us, and the other diners, alone to get on with our own lives?'

There were a few nods from the people who were still listening, and two male members of staff approached their table.

'Sir,' the smaller of the two craned his neck, looking up to Marc as he addressed him. 'Please return

42

to your table or leave the restaurant. The choice is yours.'

Marc's face started to change colour and the veins in his temple bulged as he tried to control his temper. 'It's her who should leave. I've done nothing wrong.'

'Come on, Sir, back to your table, please.'

Without warning he clenched his fist and banged it on the table. Kat's nerves were already wired, and she jumped. Jess flinched.

'This isn't the end,' he said loudly. Then he leaned towards Kat and spoke more quietly, '…it's just the beginning.' Marc then raised himself to his full height and gave the staff member a killer look. Other diners held their breath and watched, wondering what the big man was going to do next. There was a collective sigh of relief when he drew some money out of his pocket and banged it onto the table before stalking off.

'Are you all right, Madam?' asked the smaller man. 'Can I get you anything?'

Kat didn't need to look at her shaking hands to be able to answer that question. 'It was a shock, but I'll be fine. Could you get me a glass of water please?'

The excitement over for now, the restaurant got back to normal, but not for Kat and Jess. 'Shall I get the bill and we'll go back to yours?'

'Yes to the bill,' said Kat, 'but no to going back to mine. I'm not letting that man turn me into a recluse.'

'But what if we see him again, Kat? I'm worried for you?'

'I'm worried too, and that's why I'm going to the police station to report him. Then, if we still have time, we'll have our walk by the canal and look at the boats as we arranged earlier. I refuse to be a victim, Jess.'

43

'Good on you, but I'm worried. I've never seen him like that and if…'

'I know and I'm worried too. But I've changed the locks and if I ask for help from the police, I'm sure I'll be safe.'

'Okay. But if anything else happens, I think you should come and stay with us, or even your parents.'

Kat gave a wry laugh. 'There's not a chance I can stay with my parents. You know I have a great relationship with my father now and I'm so grateful that's happened, but I think me and my mother would probably end up killing each other, and I'm not sure my father's heart could take that!'

'Fair enough, Kat. But please think about coming to stay with us. I discussed it with Lucas when I first asked him, and he was fine with it.'

'I will think about it, Jess, if the situation gets any worse. But I would rather you help just after the baby's born. I know that's stretching our friendship and I don't know how Lucas would feel about having a new-born at home for a few weeks, but…'

'Of course. We've discussed that too and he agreed. He has a few visits to make to the firm's offices abroad and plans to do those late August, early September, when the schools are off and business is quieter. That means I'll be able to give you and your beautiful daughter all the love and attention you need and deserve.'

'I'm so lucky to have you and Lucas as friends, Jess. I don't know what I'd do without you.'

'Well you don't have to think about that do you, because I'm not going anywhere.'

The police were helpful and said they'd keep an eye on her apartment. She was told to call the emergency number if required, and given another number to call if Marc was making a nuisance of himself that wasn't considered an emergency.

'When will you have a word with him?' Kat asked.

'We'll find out where he's living and will send someone around,' said the officer. 'Trust me, we take this sort of behaviour very seriously and that's why we need you to keep a journal too, of when he bothers you. If necessary, we'll ask the courts for an injunction so that he can't come within a reasonable distance of you.'

'Well that was better than I expected,' Jess said when they left the police station.

'I thought so too.' Kat replied, linking arms with her friend as they headed towards the canal path.

She was shattered when she got home that evening, and slept well, despite the business with Marc earlier. Kat felt empowered, having taken action, and the support from the police made her feel a little safer. She still felt tired when she woke the following morning so made some coffee and toast and went back to bed with a book. Her phone rang shortly after she'd finished eating.

'How dare you get the police involved, you fucking bitch! You'll be sorry.' He hung up before she had a chance to respond. Kat knew he was playing with her mind, but it didn't stop her from being frightened for her own safety and that of her baby. She phoned the number given to her by the policeman.

'Okay, we'll bring him to the station this time,' she was told. It takes time to build up the evidence in these cases so keep recording dates and times in your journal for the time being, and get your phone number changed.'

She knew they had to act within the law and couldn't lock Marc away for being a nuisance. She also knew that he was playing with her head and it was unlikely that he'd do anything worse than threaten her. As much as she tried to convince herself of that, there was a little voice at the back of her mind telling her that she didn't know what her estranged husband was really capable of.

The warnings from the police must have worked because Kat didn't hear anything from Marc during the third trimester of her pregnancy, though she did still have the occasional feeling that she was being watched. She couldn't see him when she'd turned to look, and Marc was such a tall man that she convinced herself he wouldn't be able to hide. She'd been very careful to only give her new phone number to her father and close friends and hadn't received any further nasty calls from her ex.

It was the last Saturday in July and Kat threw the cover off her as she got up to use the toilet. It was still early in the morning but beads of sweat ran down her face, such was the humidity. *The hottest summer on record*, the weather forecasters had said, and it had to be while she was heavily pregnant! She was still tired but there was no point going back to bed; she couldn't get comfortable and was willing her baby to arrive as soon as possible, even though there were still two and half weeks until her due date.

The phone rang and she wondered who could be contacting her at this time in the morning.

'Your father's had a heart attack and is in intensive care,' said her mother.

'Oh My God! Is he going to be all right? How are you?'

'I'm at the hospital now. They have to do a bypass and are preparing him for theatre. It's touch and go, Katherin.' Her mother's voice broke and it was the first time Kat had heard such emotion from her.

'I'll be there as soon as I can, Mama. Give him my love.'

Kat was shaking after the call and knew she wasn't in any fit state to drive the two hours to the hospital. She phoned Jess and explained.

46

'I'll be there as soon as I can,' Jess promised.

Within thirty minutes they were heading for the hospital. Jess tried to drive as fast as she could, but had to keep them safe too. They were silent for the majority of the journey; Kat lost in her own worries and Jess just trying to get them there as best she could. The roads were busy and neither noticed that one particular car was behind them all the way from Kat's house to the hospital.

Marc was angry but not stupid, so kept his distance without losing sight of them. He had no idea where they we going but hoped the destination would be somewhere quiet.

The plan was for Jess to drop Kat off at the front of the hospital but there was a barrier and they weren't able to go that way – Jess assumed there was some sort of electronic recognition system for barriers to be raised for the ambulances, as they wouldn't have time to stop and wait. So they drove to the visitors' car park. It was large and there were plenty of spaces. She judged the hospital to be a few minutes' walk from the car park. It seemed like nothing but could be a long time when trying to get to a seriously ill relative quickly.

She parked up, and as she turned off the engine, another car parked in the space two bays from theirs. Both women were preoccupied and didn't take any notice.

As they started their hurried walk, Marc stepped out in front of them, pleased to hear Kat gasp, as she put her hand over her mouth.

'Going to deliver your little bastard, eh, Kat?'

'We're going to visit Kat's seriously ill father actually, Marc. Now get out of our way.'

'Who asked you, bitch?' he sneered, leaning towards Jess with menace in his eyes. Neither woman noticed that one hand was behind his back.

'I haven't got time for this,' said Kat, taking her phone out of her pocket and dialling the emergency police number. 'I want to report...'

Marc's hand came from behind his back lightning quick. Kat didn't finish her sentence as he thrust the knife into her chest and pulled it out. Jess watched in horror as Kat screamed in agony. She tried grabbing his arm so he couldn't stab Kat again, but he was taking no prisoners. Now in a blind rage, he vented his fury onto Jess and stabbed her repeatedly. Two brave visitors witnessed the attack and the men ran at Marc. One knocked him to the floor, but it took both of them to disarm him and to keep him still. A woman who was with one of the men called for help and doctors and nurses arrived within a minute.

It was too late. Jess was already dead, and Kat had lost both consciousness and too much blood from the stab to her heart.

'Let's see if we can save the baby,' said the female doctor and Kat was rushed to the emergency room. Less than thirty minutes later, the baby girl was taken from her now dead mother by C-Section. She was healthy, despite the traumatic start to her life.

Baby Christina lost her maternal grandfather, as well as her mother and godmother that day. When Kat's belongings had been searched and her identity discovered the hospital staff knew that telling a woman that she'd lost her daughter and husband on the same day would not be easy. They hoped she'd take some solace from the fact that she now had a beautiful granddaughter.

When she visited the baby the following day, Kat's mother waited until she was in the room alone with the child before laying her cards on the table. 'Your mother was a slut, Christina, and a disappointment to me. I'm going to make sure you don't grow up to be either.'

She cried for what should have been, and not for the loss of her daughter or husband, and gave the baby her surname, her daughter's maiden name.

Chapter 3 – The Witch

Rotating his head one hundred and eighty degrees, the praying mantis looked out from the two bulging eyes at the side of his triangular head. His binocular field of vision caught movement in the grass and he moved slowly towards his prey, focusing on the moving moth while the rest of the area around him blurred into insignificance. The moth had no chance as the mantis struck. Grabbing the creature with his spiked raptorial forelegs, he bit the still struggling insect and slowly devoured it while it was still alive. After satisfying his hunger, he checked out his body.

So this time I'm male, thought the Witch as she slowly got used to the body she occupied, knowing that, like all of her other reincarnation experiences, it wasn't going to have a happy ending. She was on the Merry-go-round of Satan's wrath and this was just the latest punishment for disobeying his orders during her last human life. Despite the grim situation, the Witch was a maverick and, try as she might, she knew she couldn't change her nature. *Next time I'll make more of an effort.* She vowed to get on the best side of her master in the future if she was ever fortunate enough to possess a human mind and body again, like an addict trying to convince herself, more than anyone else. All thought of future lives stopped as a female praying mantis moved in the distance, and the Witch experienced an overwhelming desire to copulate.

They skirted around each other for a few seconds before the Witch cautiously approached the larger female. The female raised herself to tower over him and the Witch had no doubt who would be in charge of the proceedings. Before he knew it, she had lifted him onto her back. He tentatively twisted his abdomen and attached to her. His host didn't object so he got down to business. As he started to empty his sperm packets into the obliging female, she rotated her big head and looked at him with a hunger that had nothing to do with sexual desire. Before the Witch knew what was happening, the female's large mouth had engulfed his head. There was a sharp pain and she decapitated him in one bite. His body continued to ejaculate without its head. Then he died, still attached to the back of the female. The larger insect continued to feast on the male and, once replete, she carried on about her business without a care in the world. The soul of the Witch now watched from above with both fascination and admiration for the creature, hoping that in future, she could replicate the success of the female praying mantis but in the body of a female human.

The Witch waited for the hands of Satan's slaves to take her back to Hell and wondered what savage punishments were next in store for her. The hands didn't appear. She realised there could be a chance for her to return as a human but knew it was only a matter of time before the demons came for her and she'd have to be quick. Too weak and out of practice to possess an adult, the Witch moved quickly to hunt for her prey. She found the ideal host. Determined to make her next life as long and enjoyable as she could, she threw herself into the mind and body of the screaming baby and decided to bide her time.

*****

Mrs Jansen first noticed something strange during Christina's Baptism. She knew her granddaughter could go from angelic to screaming like a banshee at the flick of a switch, but that wasn't a reason for anyone to look at the baby as if she were the spawn of Satan. When she handed Christina to the priest, he smiled and looked down at the child. His face then turned ashen as he saw a brief glimpse of

51

something in the baby's eyes and she felt the need to ask him if he was all right.

'It's a joyous occasion and I'm fine, Mrs Jansen,' he responded, but she wasn't convinced he was telling the truth. *But there again,* she wondered, *why on earth would a man of the cloth lie, especially while in God's own house?*

Christina started crying as soon as he held her. When the priest uttered the words, 'I baptise you in the name of the Father…,' she screamed her lungs out and didn't stop until they left the church.

Her grandmother had a bad feeling throughout the whole ceremony and needed to speak to the priest in private, but Christina's screaming set her nerves on edge and she could tell by their expressions that everyone in the church felt the same way – it would have to keep until she was alone.

She arranged for a fellow Women's Institute member to babysit Christina the following Wednesday, and made her way to see the priest as pre-arranged.

'How can I help you?' he asked.

'I saw the way you looked at Christina, Father. What was wrong?'

He gave her a benevolent smile. 'Nothing my child, nothing at all.'

'But, Father, I…'

'Mrs Jansen, your granddaughter looked the spitting image of the child I baptised in my first ceremony some years ago,' he lied. 'It took me back to how young I was, and how nervous I was then during my first ceremony. I'm sorry if my reaction unsettled you.'

'Oh thank you, Father. I was so worried.'

'Nothing to worry about, my child. Will we see you on Sunday?'

'Of course, Father.'

The priest didn't anticipate that she would bring the baby with her and that the *demon child,* as he came to think of Christina, would cry from the moment she was brought into the church until she left. He hoped with all of his heart that God's goodness would rid the child of the demon, but was ashamed to admit his fears, even of one so young.

Her grandmother tried on a number of occasions to take Christina to church with her, but the reaction was always the same. She changed her own worship day to Wednesday, knowing one of the WI members would babysit. She resented her granddaughter's behaviour; for making her give up church on a Sunday. She resolved to return as soon as the child was old enough to be punished for misbehaving.

*****

From a young age, it was normal for Christina to have two voices in her head. Hers was the first, and the second belonged to the 'naughty girl' who had started to call herself Witch. Witch could take over her mind and make her body do things that Christina didn't want to. She always knew when Witch wanted to do something because Christina's head started pounding. She'd already had loads of tests, but nobody could find anything wrong.

'Let's break Oma's lady, Christina,' said Witch one day.

'Noooooo, Oma will be upset. She loves lady.'

'Oma's horrible. She calls your mum a slut. That's a bad word and Oma doesn't deserve you.'

'Oma loves me!'

'No she doesn't. She's going to put you in a home. She hates you because you're a bastard.'

'She doesn't hate me!...What's a bastard?'

'She hates you. She hates you. She hates you.'

53

As much as Christina tried to fight against Witch's voice in her head, it dominated more and more each day. If she did what Witch told her to, the awful pain and pounding in her head would go away for a while. She tried hard not to pick up the ornament of the Virgin Mary, knowing how much her grandmother loved it, but Witch was stronger.

'Who are you talking to, Christina?' asked Mrs Jensen, coming into the room from the kitchen. 'Oh no!' she said as her eyes darted to what her granddaughter held in her hands and she gasped. The beautiful child was standing in the corner of the room, the ringlets of her long blonde hair framing her oval-shaped face, and her big blue eyes glaring at her grandmother in anger. It was like another person was looking at her from the eyes of her granddaughter's; Mrs Jensen could always tell by her eyes; they softened suddenly, and the child lowered the ornament as if she was about to put it down. Her grandmother exhaled a huge breath, sighing with relief, but it was short lived. The cruelty returned to Christina's eyes and she pulled her arm back, as if to throw the Virgin Mary icon. Putting her hands in the prayer position, she tried to reason with the five-year-old. 'Put the Virgin Mary down, Christina, there's a good girl.'

'I am a good girl, Oma, but Witch is a naughty girl.'

'I know, Christina. Tell Witch she'll get into trouble if she breaks the Virgin Mary. Now put it down, this instant.'

'I won't put it down. Watch this.'

The child's expression and voice had changed and looking into her granddaughter's eyes, Mrs Jensen knew she was now looking at a demon. She was convinced of what she had suspected almost since the day Christina was born. The child was possessed. Mrs Jensen knelt down and prayed with all her heart and

54

soul. The sound of the ornament shattering into pieces caused her to stop for a brief second. Then she ignored everything around her again and prayed to the Lord God, asking for forgiveness for her sins and the sins of her daughter and for help with the child. She felt calmer after she'd spoken to God and knew what she must do.

Ignoring questions and comments from both Christina and Witch, Mrs Jensen packed towels and a complete change of clothes for Christina, pushed the child's arms into her coat sleeves, pulled on her own, and headed for the tram stop. Less than an hour later, she was about to enter the church.

'I'm not going in there.'

Mrs Jensen knew this was the Witch's voice and she tightened her grip. 'You are coming with me, child, and the priest is going to get rid of you, demon!'

A few pedestrians watched as the old woman dragged the young girl, kicking and screaming, up the church path. She stopped screaming as they entered the church and looked around her with a sneer on her face. The priest walked towards them. He was the same ashen colour as he had been when Christina had been baptised.

'You knew then,' Mrs Jensen said. 'Didn't you?'

'I suspected, Mrs Jensen,' he replied. 'But didn't want to believe it.'

'Hello, Father,' said Witch, the words holding a sinister tone that no mere child could manifest.

Both adults shivered involuntarily.

'Sit down, child,' said the priest, and was surprised when Christina did as she'd been told. 'Let us pray.' He bowed his head.

The child got up from the pew and leaning her face towards the priest's bowed head, laughed openly in his face. She then curtsied and started to skip around

55

the church, touching items as she did so and pretending to be hurt.

'Ouch,' she said, after bending down to touch a prayer cushion. 'My hand's burnt.' She looked at her hand. 'Oh, just kidding, it's not really.' She picked up the cushion and threw it at the priest. It bounced off his shoulder, and he stuttered for a second, before deciding to finish his prayers.

The Witch didn't like being ignored so skipped around the church, looking for something sturdier to throw at the Bible Basher.

'Bishop Lange will be here shortly. He's authorised to carry out exorcisms once he's satisfied that it is demonic possession and not some sort of mental illness,' the priest said once prayers were over.

'I know she's possessed, Father, but what if he doesn't believe me?'

'I've already spoken to him and explained the situation. He believes me but has to see for himself. As long as the child speaks in both voices, there is absolutely no doubt.'

They turned their heads at the sound of the door opening, and in walked a very tall man wearing the robes of his office.

Christina skipped towards him. 'Ooh, another one,' she said, 'but this one's the boss. Hello, Bishop.'

The bishop ignored the child. He turned the key in the church door, locking them all in, then walked up the aisle towards the priest and Mrs Jansen, Witch skipping around him, trying to get his attention.

'Christina!' called Mrs Jansen.

'Yes, Oma.' This time it was Christina who answered. 'Witch won't go away, Oma. She doesn't like it here and wants to go home.'

'Come here, Christina.'

'Make me!' Witch answered.

Having now heard both voices, the bishop's face set. 'I wondered whether this child had the extremely rare condition of juvenile schizophrenia,' he said, 'but this appears to be a genuine demonic possession. Has she seen a doctor?'

'Yes, and we have an appointment with a specialist next month. They think it's schizophrenia but it's unusual in one so young. She also has severe headaches which they can't do anything about. We all know there's a demon. It doesn't surprise me, knowing her mother's behaviour.'

'Let's get started,' said the bishop, ignoring Mrs Jansen's last comment.

For such a large man who was encumbered by the clothes of his office, he moved very fast. The bishop grabbed Christina and, carrying her under one arm, made his way to the front of the church. The child kicked and screamed, then started cursing, using words that Mrs Jansen had seldom heard in her whole life.

'You son of a fucking bastard and a whore,' Witch screeched, screwing up her face.

Mrs Jansen watched in horror as her granddaughter's face screwed even tighter, almost as though she were bearing down. It soon became apparent that she was defecating. The stench filled the church and, despite the strong hold the bishop had on her, Christina managed to wriggle out of his arms. Laughing, she stood in front of him, then deliberately thrust her hand down the back of her knickers. Her grandmother's world went into slow motion as the big turd hit her straight in the face. Excrement went up her nose and into her mouth. She tried desperately to keep her mouth shut despite wanting to both scream and ring the child's neck. Fighting against gagging at the smell and taste of the faeces, Mrs Jansen took the towel out of her bag and wiped the worst of the mess off her face. She then hurried as fast as she could to the door at

57

the back of the main church hall, all the time trying not to vomit, accompanied by the sound of her granddaughter who was now laughing hysterically. She opened the door to the back room and closed it quickly behind her to block out the sound. She scrubbed her face properly in the bathroom and took a few deep breaths, trying to calm her nerves as best she could. She didn't want to go back to the church hall, but knew she had to. She drew a deep breath and opened the door.

The bishop and the priest had removed Christina's soiled clothes and had tied her to a chair. The child was now crying, and it seemed to Mrs Jansen that Witch had left and Christina was back, albeit temporarily.

'Do you have fresh clothes for her?' the bishop asked. 'We don't want the child to suffer more than she has to.'

'Oma, Oma,' said Christina. 'I'm frightened, Oma, and cold. Help me, please. Don't let them hurt me.'

Mrs Jansen ignored the child's pleas and wiped the mess off the skin she could see with a cloth she had dampened in the bathroom. She popped a dress over Christina's head, aware of the fact that the child was still partly soiled, but unable to do anything about it for the time being. The bishop was praying and ignoring the others. As soon as she was dressed, the child screwed up her face and Mrs Jansen knew that Witch was back, before she uttered a word.

The bishop stood to face the three. The child writhed against her restraints and the bishop picked up a bowl and dipped his fingers into the holy water. Walking around Christina, he splashed her with it.

'Demon, I command you! Retreat from this child.'

Christina bucked up and down on the chair, the demon Witch clearly unhappy with the proceedings. The bishop ignored her as he recited the Lord's Prayer and the Hail Mary; the beginning of the exorcism rituals issued by the Vatican. He had completed an exorcism course and been called upon on two other occasions, but both of these had been for adults whose demons were not as strong as the one in this child.

At the end of the proceedings the child slumped down in her seat.

'Is it over?' asked Mrs Jansen. 'Has she gone?'

'I hope so,' said the bishop, but he wasn't convinced. He put a comforting hand on Mrs Jansen's forearm. 'Success isn't guaranteed the first time. Sometimes it can take days, weeks, or months of prayer and further exorcisms. But we will prevail, with the Lord's help.'

'Weeks or months? You mean that this could go on for *weeks*, even *months*, and you have no idea how long it will take?'

'We won't know until the child wakes up. She's exhausted and is going to need all the love and attention you can give her.'

'Love and attention after what's happened here today? And knowing how her mother turned out? No. I can't do this.'

'I know it's frightening, Mrs Jansen, but the Lord will give us strength through these difficult times and Christina will eventually be free of her demon.'

'I can't. I can't do this.' She looked at the bishop, then at the priest, and finally at her sleeping granddaughter. 'It's never going to end; I just know it. And I can't look after her anymore.'

She left the church and none of them ever saw her again.

*****

The priest contacted the social services and Christina was placed in a children's home. Her medical appointments were delayed but, after many rounds of appointments and a number of counselling sessions, she was finally diagnosed with early onset schizophrenia at age six. This was rare and unusual for a child so young, as the condition usually presented itself in adolescents or young adults, but having carried out all of the tests and spoken extensively to the child, the specialists were convinced that this was the correct diagnosis, and prescribed drugs to help with the condition. Nobody suggested getting in contact with the church, and when the priest made enquiries on the orders of the bishop, he was informed that information about Christina's whereabouts could not be divulged to the church to protect her rights and for data protection reasons.

Christina had a troubled childhood not only because of Witch but also because of her looks. She was a charming and thoughtful child when on her own and anyone she met found it hard to believe that such a pleasant and beautiful-looking child could turn into a monster at the flick of a switch. As she grew older, girls became jealous of her looks, but those who were cruel to her were paid back in spades; sometimes Witch pinched or punched them when no-one else was looking, at other times she discovered her tormentors' worst nightmares, and her threats revolved around these. Even those who had once felt sorry for the nasty girl, learned to give her a wide berth. Fellow pupils avoided her, and Christina got used to her own company, and a life without love.

Throughout her adolescence, various foster homes were found for the child, two with a view to eventually adopting her. But Witch always made an appearance and ruined everything for Christina. 'We don't need anyone else,' she always told her host.

Despite hating her, Christina was unable to do anything to get rid of her although she tried many times, often putting herself and others in danger in the

60

process. Her medication was changed when she stepped in front of a tram in a bid to end her life, but was saved by a local citizen.

Occasionally, a cruel and stupid child would decide to pick on Christina, never dreaming there would be consequences to their actions.

'You're crazy and you have the devil in you,' said Ruben Groot, the biggest boy in her class, one day. It hurt Christina and as the tears ran down her cheeks, the boy wondered why others were frightened of her. He found out during the school morning break when Christina complained of a pounding headache and Witch decided to pay him a visit while he was having a sneaky cigarette with two friends.

Without saying a word, she walked towards the three boys.

'Should I be frightened,' he said to his friends. 'Look, I'm shaking.' They all laughed.

'You will be,' she said, gripping the wrist that wasn't holding the cigarette, and the laughter soon stopped. He used all of his strength to try to loosen her grip, but Witch had him in a vice-like hold and he couldn't remove her hand. As he struggled, she snatched the cigarette out of his other hand. 'This is what happens when you're not nice to me,' she said, pressing the burning cigarette end onto his lower arm.

'Aaarrrggghh,' the boy screamed out in pain. 'You are fucking mad!'

'That I am, and don't you forget it.' She laughed, worthy of a superhero villain. 'I'll come for you all if you tell any teachers about this,' she said, then threw back her long blonde hair and stalked off, leaving the bully writhing in agony and his friends in awe and fear of the beautiful teenager who was absolutely crazy.

The bishop who had tried to exorcise the demon from Christina had managed to track her down and had discreetly kept a track of her movements. He'd

61

sent the priest to the home where she lived on many occasions, but nobody listened. The bishop recalled the fear seen in the priest's eyes those twelve years before and knew his heart wasn't in it. The man was a coward and a shame to his calling. The bishop was determined to deal with the demon and to exorcise it so the girl would eventually have a chance of a normal life.

He made an appointment to see the manager of the children's home. 'I tried to exorcise the demon from Christina Jansen when the child was three years old,' he told the man. 'Her grandmother was terrified and disappeared without trace, and that's when the child was put into a home. She...'

'I'm well aware of the situation, er, Bishop, but...'

'It's Your Excellency.'

'Pardon?'

'My office is addressed as Your Excellency, and not Bishop. But I'm happy for...'

'I see. Well it's like this, *Your Excellency*...' The manager leaned forward and sarcastically emphasised the words. 'The priest has already been to see me, and I told him exactly what I'm about to tell you. Christina Jansen is a schizophrenic. She's been diagnosed by trained doctors who have studied for years to be able to make that diagnosis. I'm not having any child under my care subjected to archaic customs and ceremonies that could...no-*would*, scar them for life. Now if there's nothing else, Your Excellency?'

The bishop left without further discussion. He prayed for the soul of the children's home manager that evening and, knowing there was more than one way to skin a cat, asked the Lord for guidance. The following morning, he arranged to visit the school Christina attended.

The Lord does indeed work in mysterious ways, the bishop acknowledged when the head teacher fawned over him.

'It's an honour and a privilege to have you at our humble school, Your Excellency,' she said as she shook his hand. 'How can I help you?'

'I've come to talk about a child named Christina Jansen. You know her?'

'Ah,' said the head teacher. 'I know Christina very well, and for all the wrong reasons. Hers is a sad story but it's sometimes difficult to feel sorry for the girl, even knowing what she's been through.'

'I know she's been diagnosed with schizophrenia,' said the bishop, 'but there's more to it than that. The girl is possessed, and I need to carry out the Lord's work to rid her of the demon.'

'And how would you propose to do this, Your Excellency? If Christina is, indeed, possessed, I can't imagine she would give her permission for her demons to be exorcised.'

'You are right, of course. But I wouldn't be doing my duty if I didn't try, and it will be easier with your help.'

'If I was to agree to this, Your Excellency, how do you propose we would proceed?'

'Leave that to me…'

The following week Christina received a letter informing her that she was to be under the care of a new psychiatrist and that an appointment had been arranged. Knowing there would be hassle if she didn't attend, she informed the school and made arrangements to go to the surgery. This one was in an area she wasn't familiar with, and she was nervous when she got off the bus and followed the directions on the appointment card.

She'd been under different specialists all of her life but never knowing when Witch was likely to

63

appear, or what she would do, always made Christina nervous. As a youngster, it used to be that she had no idea what had happened when Witch took over her mind and body, but now Witch would sometimes tell her what was required or what she planned to do. The pounding in Christina's head was not so painful when she didn't fight the demon and Christina wasn't sure if knowing what was going to happen was better or worse. Sometimes she recalled parts of what had happened when Witch had taken over, like a drunk's memories slowly coming back as they sobered up.

She arrived at the given address and looked up at the house. Something didn't feel right and she felt the hairs on the back of her neck standing up, in warning. About to turn around and run, the door opened before Christina rang the bell.

'Christina Jansen?' asked a big man who looked nothing like a doctor's receptionist.

She was about to say yes, when Witch decided to take over. 'No,' her voice growled. Desperate for help and hoping there may be some random demons in the ether who would welcome a fight, Witch summoned up her powers and called, 'Help me.'

There was a change in the atmosphere and a blast of air blew. The front door slammed shut, locking out the man and Christina. Witch laughed and was about to turn around to leave when the big man looked up and down the quiet street and, satisfied that nobody was in the vicinity, grabbed her wrist in a vice-like grip.

'Noooooooo!' she shouted.

The man quickly rang the bell before putting his other hand over her mouth. The door was answered by another man with muscles that would be the envy of the largest silverback gorilla.

Witch's strength was unnatural, and both men worked hard to restrain her, taking punches and enduring bites into the process. She screamed, spat and kicked out, but they eventually got her into a room in which a single chair rested at its centre. They manhandled her over to it and forced her into the seat.

'Her neck,' the first man said, and his colleague squeezed his hand around Witch's neck as the other man attempted to tie the restraints.

Her attention diverted to her neck and she now expended all her energy on trying to relieve the pressure of his hands. This gave them the time they needed to secure her to the chair, and her neck was released as soon as the job was done. Witch summoned all of her strength and tested the restraints. They didn't budge and she knew she couldn't do this on her own.

Looking around the room, her eyes landed on the large cross on the wall and she felt her skin start to burn. Hissing, she looked away from it. The bad feeling she'd felt outside worsened and she knew she had to summon help. Trying to keep calm, she closed her eyes and spoke her thoughts.

'I call on all Satan's Demons. Help me to…'

The door opened and her summons stopped midstream as she opened her eyes again. The holy men in front of her were dressed in the robes of their office and she remembered the one dressed in purple from years before, when Christina had been a child.

She didn't recognise the priest but watched as he picked up a vessel and prayed over it before crossing the vessel and then crossing himself. He handed the vessel to the bishop.

'Hurry,' she thought. 'Get me out of here.'

The bishop held the vessel in front of him and prayed to his Lord asking for protection before requesting help to rid the girl of the evil spirit. He walked around the chair and Witch tried lunging at him.

The bishop nodded to one of the men who held onto the back of the chair so it wouldn't move and then

65

walked round the chair, chanting. As he dipped his hands in the water, she screamed. The first drops he splashed at her hit her neck. The holy men and their heavies all gasped as the flesh on her neck sizzled and two small, bright red marks appeared where the water drops had hit.

The other men in the room looked to the bishop for guidance. The bishop was keeping a calm expression though he thought his heart would explode out of his chest. He glimpsed fear in the girl's eyes and knew he had the upper hand. He doubled his efforts. Witch writhed in her chair, despite the man at the back of her, trying to guess when he was going to splash the next lot of water so she could avoid it landing on her skin. At the same time, she called silently for other demons to help.

She felt tired and knew she'd have to leave Christina's body if she didn't get help soon. They'd put a layer of protection around her host and she knew it would be difficult to get back in. This was the best host she'd been in and she enjoyed the novelty of physical beauty and the way that boys and men already reacted to this beauty, even though it wasn't yet fully developed. No, they weren't getting rid of her that easily.

As the bishop carried on his incantations Christina's body jerked, then became completely still. Everything in the room stopped and the bishop and his new priest looked at each other. The priest allowed himself a smile and the two big men relaxed, the tension visibly disappearing from their shoulders. About to speak, the bishop wondered if he was the only one to feel the strangeness.

'It's not over.' As soon as the words left his mouth there was a whirling sound, as if a wind had suddenly whipped up from nowhere. They watched in sickly awe as what appeared to be mini tornados appeared in the four corners of the room. A true force of nature, they swirled together as they formed into one above Christina's head. She looked up and smiled, and then they shot down into her body through her mouth.

The big men crossed themselves and the priest fell to his knees. The bishop trembled and tried to gather strength from the Lord and his faith.

'Leave her, spawn of Satan,' he shouted, and was about to accompany his words with a splash of water on the girl when an invisible force stopped his hand. As hard as he tried, the pressure on his arm was such that it was stuck in mid-air, and he couldn't move it up or down.

'No!' screamed Witch, opening her eyes and looking directly into the bishop's. 'I'm not going anywhere.'

'Oh, yes you are,' said the bishop. 'Lord, by all the things that are holy, help us to rid this child and this room of these evil demons.'

The other men in the room started moving around, twitching or jumping as they were hit or pushed, and punching out at invisible enemies. The bishop could see that demons were trying to control his helpers as well as the girl in the chair. Apart from using their strength on his arm, they weren't doing anything else to him and he doubled his efforts, beseeching the Lord God to save their mortal bodies and their souls.

Christina let out an almighty roar that silenced all other activity within the room for a few seconds. They watched in horror as her face contorted as she put pressure on her constraints and the heavy rope frayed, as if it were merely a decorative bow on a Christmas gift. But this wasn't Christmas and Witch certainly wasn't a gift. Bursting out of her restraints, she roared and screamed obscenities for the injustices of all her past lives, and for the humiliation the bishop wanted to inflict on her in this one. Laced with venom, the words were enough to instil fear into each of the men and they would have fled, had they been able. All except the bishop. He didn't know how he summoned the strength, but suddenly it felt as if a different invisible source was fighting the first one and he could move again. He chanted words that were unfamiliar, and a calmness descended over him.

The air shuddered again, and more tornadoes whirled around, battering into each other above the men who watched, dumb struck.

Witch took two steps towards the man who had choked her.

'Get ready to go to Hell.' A man's voice came out of the girl, and the bishop's aide wet himself.

About to take the last step towards the man, she suddenly stopped. Her face turned bright red with the effort of moving but she was stuck to the spot unable to move.

'Go!' shouted the Bishop. 'The three of you.'

The priest and one of the burly aides didn't need telling twice and disappeared from the room as if being chased by the four horses of the apocalypse. Not so the aide that Witch wanted to throttle.

'I'm not leaving you, Your Excellency.'

The bishop could see the fear in his eyes but admired the man's bravery.

'Leave now!'

'No!' He was adamant, and it gave the bishop renewed strength.

'Come to me,' the bishop said, and his aide obeyed.

The bishop felt the words in his head and knew he was being guided by an invisible force of good. His resolute faith didn't need to ask questions and he did as ordered, holding out his hands to his aide. The man shrugged his shoulders and gave him a confused look.

'Hold my hands,' he said. 'Quickly, and do everything I tell you, no matter what.'

The aide nodded and held the bishop's hands, and without knowing what they were doing or why, they unwittingly formed their own circle of love.

The fight went on all around them and when goodness was weakened and Witch was able to move again, she encountered an invisible barrier between herself and the men she wanted to throttle. Her face contorted and the beauty of Christina deformed first into that of a pock-ridden old man, then to the face of one of the devil's underlings, and finally to that of a middle-aged haggard Witch with rotting teeth and a mouth permanently turned down at the edges. The aide stared at her, mesmerized, like a rabbit in the headlights, and the bishop felt his grip loosening.

'Concentrate,' said the firm but gentle voice in his head. *'Concentrate and close your eyes. We will overcome!'*

He felt loved. Despite the chaos and devilry with them in that room, the bishop felt the most overwhelming sense of love that he'd ever felt in his whole life. And he knew, without doubt, that the Lord and his angels would win the battle on this day.

'Close your eyes, my child,' he said to his aide, 'and hold on tight. They can't hurt us today and we will overcome.'

The aide felt the power of love that accompanied the words and his fear was replaced by calmness. They stood, eyes closed and praying as the battle continued around them. Neither had any idea how long it was before the door slamming brought them out of their semi-trance and the bishop felt the change in the atmosphere. He opened his eyes, knowing that both evil and the greater good had now left.

'We're safe,' he said, and his aide opened his eyes. He let go of one of the hands of the bishop but they both still needed the comfort of another human as they looked around the room. Vomit covered one of the walls and faeces another. They'd removed the ornaments before Christina had arrived, but the one chair and sideboard lay in tatters on the floor, as did the landscape pictures that had hung on the walls. The only item that was no worse for wear was the large cross, still hanging on the wall and shining like a beacon at the end of a dark tunnel.

'I'll clean up, Your Excellency.'

'I'll help you,' said the bishop. 'We're in this together.'

The aide didn't argue and, as they set about righting the room, both men knew they now shared a bond that would never be broken.

Witch had to get away. She ran from the house in a panic knowing that a battle was going on in the other world, but not knowing whether she would be safe or taken. As the scar already forming on her neck throbbed and burned her skin, memories of another life and the way it had ended came rushing back; memories that she thought she'd suppressed for eternity. Her eyes wide open, she looked like a startled deer as she ran blindly, trying to remove the picture from her mind's eye. But she couldn't shake it off. She was tied to the stake and hearing the bloodthirsty villagers shouting. *'Burn the Witch! Burn the Witch.'* She had screamed for mercy but was shown none as the village elder lit the wood at her feet. Centuries had passed but Witch could still smell first the wood, and then the smell of her own flesh burning, like a suckling pig at the lord of the manor's festival. She stopped running and fell to the floor.

'Are you all right, dear? Can you sit up?'

Christina opened her eyes and looked into the eyes of the old woman who had spoken to her. Before she could answer, two younger men approached.

Sitting up, she looked at the three people surrounding her. 'I guess I must have fainted, but I feel fine now, thanks,' she said, trying to stand but unsteady on her feet.

'Here, have some water.'

She took an unopened bottle one of the men held out towards her, opened it and took a grateful slurp. Handing it back, she thanked them again and went on her way. Her neck was throbbing, and Christina tried to recall what had happened, initially without success. It started to come back to her later when she was alone in her room, and she was nauseous for the rest of that night and the entirety of the following day, accompanied by a headache from hell itself.

Naturally, the head teacher enquired about her whereabouts. The home manager informed her that Christina was having a migraine episode and would be back to school as soon as she could.

When she returned to school (and unbeknown to her), Christina's movements were monitored and her actions reported back to the head teacher. She was a model student for the next three days. The head teacher phoned the bishop at the end of the third day. It was always lovely to be able to give good news on a Friday.

'Whatever you did has worked so far. The bad girl hasn't made an appearance since the…the appointment with you.'

'That's good news,' the bishop hesitated,' but be careful. I know this isn't the end of it and it's not going to be easy to rid the girl of her demons for good.'

'Yes, Your Excellency.' She smiled after finishing the call. The bishop was being over-cautious and modest about his own abilities. Christina would be fine now and the head vowed to give extra thanks during her prayers in church on Sunday.

*****

Christina opened her eyes on Sunday morning after a peaceful night's sleep and smiled to herself. Tuesday to Sunday marked the longest she'd been without a visit from Witch and her headache had gone. She felt the mark on her neck again and was amazed at how hot it still felt to her touch, but there was no longer the throbbing pain she'd first felt after coming around from the faint. The memories of the bishop's exorcism again played out in her mind in fits and starts, and she was glad she'd been absent during the horrendous event. She lay back in bed, daring to wonder what a life would be like without Witch inside her head.

As Christina got up to use the bathroom, she felt a sharp pain in her forehead and closed her right eye.

A voice entered her head. *'I'm back,'* it said, and she knew her optimism had been misplaced, and she'd never know a life alone with her own thoughts. *'We need money, our own place, and we don't need an interfering bishop.'*

Christina cried like a baby at the hand fate had thrown at her.

'Oh, did Christina want to be all alone?' For the rest of the day, Witch dripped venom into her head with comments that ate away at her self esteem. Exhausted from the events of the day, she was grateful to feel sleep taking over, the only place where the demon didn't yet visit her.

Witch had a plan and it involved a more than usual active presence within Christina. She soon realised her host was being watched in school, so tried to rein in her natural tendencies to cause chaos because she was aware the bishop would be notified, and they might try to repeat the process. The exorcism attempt had weakened her and each time she fought for supremacy over Christina it drained her. She had to conserve energy for her longer active visits and to carry out her plan. She shuddered at the memory of the event with the bishop and his sycophantic lackeys, and was even more determined to get him out of her life once and for all. Having toyed with, and dismissed, a number of ideas, she had a eureka moment; it now seemed obvious that this was the way ahead, especially in this day and age when people were more likely to believe youngsters than a man of the cloth.

She looked around the classroom trying to recall the religion of the other kids when they'd had their Religious Studies class. As she looked at the three boys who had tried to torment her before, and at Ruben, the one she had burnt with the cigarette, Witch smiled. She was pleased to see the fear in the eyes of all three.

With a little help from Ruben it hadn't taken much effort to discover that the bishop was conducting the services at St Margaret's Church until a new priest was recruited for the diocese. He'd also told her that rumour was, something had traumatised the priest, who was on sick leave pending a decision about his future. Attendance at the church had increased while the bishop took the services, and Witch already knew that the head teacher had encouraged attendance from a number of teenagers at their school. Having looked at the place from a distance, she could see for herself that the congregation had grown since word was out that the bishop was taking the services.

Witch wasn't surprised to discover that Ruben was a great snitch. The boy was a bully and bullies were generally weak cowards. He'd heard a conversation between the bishop and their head teacher.

'While I thank the Lord for bringing in more worshippers,' the bishop had said, 'I expect attendance to revert to pitiful normality when the new priest arrives. But it'll do for now, and the extra money will go some way to filling the coffers and for paying for the room in the house to be repaired. It was like a hurricane had ripped through it, causing complete destruction.'

She smiled at the memory of asking Ruben what had happened and in which house.

'I don't know where it was, just that something otherworldly and awful had happened.'

'Did they say anything else?' Witch asked.

'The bishop said they'd have to find a new venue for the next one and the head said something about having warned him and not wanting anything to do with it. She didn't even call him Your Excellency - so, what's all this about, Christina?'

'You'll find out, Ruben, all in good time.'

She was pleased that he'd helped so far, but knew she'd have to use a little more persuasion to guarantee his further involvement in her plan, which was twofold.

While the service was taking place the following Sunday, she visited the bishop's residence on the outskirts of the town in the heart of the diocese.

The modest sized house was off a quiet country road and surrounded by hedges, so members of the public couldn't see inside. Nobody was about as she approached the front door and brazenly rang the bell. No answer. She walked around the property and found no evidence of CCTV cameras. Witch wasn't surprised; this was a respectable town area with a low crime rate.

At the back of the property there was a separate outhouse. Before touching anything, she put on a pair of latex gloves, then tried the door and it opened. Inside, she was surprised to find various tools and some sort of half-made wooden cupboard. *So the bishop enjoyed making things*. On the window ledge stood a painted wooden statue of Christ. Witch felt rage run through her as she looked at the icon. Without conscious thought she reached up for it and threw it to the floor. The statue landed face-up, undamaged and she thought the eyes bored into her as she looked at it. She closed her own, trying to gain control of her feelings and realising he might suspect her if she destroyed anything religious. It took tremendous willpower for her to pick it up, wipe off the dust, and replace it on the window ledge. She felt sick and wanted to get out of there as soon as possible. She looked around as quickly as she could and noticed a plant pot in the corner of the workshop that looked out of place. A sixth sense told her to lift it. She found a key underneath and smiled as she left the workshop and entered the bishop's residence through the back door.

Avoiding any further distraction, she quickly found the bishop's study and searched his desk until she found what she was looking for. Already adept, and with a rare natural talent with numbers, she studied the bishop's ledgers. The writing in the margins matched that of other paperwork in the desk drawers so she quickly established that he did his own accounting, or at least part of it. There was a separate book for each of the churches within the diocese. Witch concentrated on the accounts for St Margaret's Church and got to work. The accounts were organised into calendar years and she worked back over the previous five years, randomly ensuring that the incoming columns showed a greater number than outgoings, so none of the figures matched. She worked quickly, knowing she had a maximum of two hours, and that included time for the bishop to conduct the service and to chat with the parishioners. Recalling where everything went, she returned the books and then took three pieces of the diocese headed paper out of the second drawer, together with matching envelopes.

Everything back where it should be, she left the house, locked up and returned the key to its place in the outhouse. She walked away and watched from the corner of the street for a while, to see what time he returned, so she knew how long she would have for her visit the following Sunday. Fifteen minutes later, a woman arrived and let herself into the house. His housekeeper or chef, Witch presumed, wondering whether she could incriminate any of his staff into the plan. *Stick to your original ideas,* she told herself as she made her way back to her room at the home, looking forward to school the following day and seeing the look on the face of Ruben when she told him what he must do, or the consequences he would suffer.

Christina turned up for school the following day and enjoyed the peace she felt at being alone in her own head. She smiled at her fellow classmates and said hello to them but wasn't surprised when some just grunted back a 'hi', and the braver of her classmates ignored her completely. They all gave her a wide berth. Having seen her change from nice to nasty at a flick of a switch, they were understandably wary. Christina had learnt to live with this but on the rare occasions she was alone in her head, she felt an overwhelming sense of loneliness, and wondered if this was how the rest of her life would pan out. The thought of finding like-minded people to spend time with terrified her and, with a sigh, she knew she would just have to get used to being on her own.

It was almost a relief to have company when Witch entered her head. And then she told her what she wanted her to do, and Christina acknowledged, not for the first time, that Witch was actually pure evil and very dangerous.

'*I'm not doing that!*' Christina slammed a hand on her desk.

'Are you all right, Christina?' the maths teacher asked, seeing the obvious distress on Christina's face.

The students sitting near her fidgeted, showing their discomfort. They all knew she was schizophrenic and most had experienced the other side of her, none of the experiences pleasant.

'Sorry, Miss Zoe. Can I be excused for a few minutes?'

'Yes, of course.'

Christina left the class and Miss Zoe told the other students to carry on with their studies. A minute or so later she addressed them again and told them she had to leave them alone for a few minutes. 'Keep studying quietly and I'll be back as soon as I can,' she said, as she left the classroom and headed straight to the head teacher's office.

'You can't go in there,' Maria, the school secretary said. 'She's on the phone.'

The maths teacher took no notice and walked straight in. The head calmly carried on her conversation and indicated with her hand that Zoe should take a seat.

'I tried to stop her,' Maria said, as soon as the call was finished.

'It's fine, Maria. Now Zoe, what's so urgent that you come barging into my office when Maria tells you I'm busy?'

Satisfied that the teacher had been put in her place, Maria left the head's room, closing the door behind her.

'She's back,' Zoe said, and the head felt the sunshine disappear as a cloud of darkness descended upon her.

Chapter 4 – Bye Bye Bishop

Used to acting quickly on her decisions, Witch found it a long wait until the following Sunday but knew she had to be patient for her plan to succeed. To take her mind off waiting, she typed a letter on her laptop and, when the office in the home was quiet, printed out three different versions, each with a different address, onto the headed paper she'd stolen from the bishop's residence. She finished each letter with the phrase; *from a concerned, anonymous member of staff.*

The next Sunday, when she went to the bishop's residence, there was activity inside and she had to wait until the woman who she'd seen the last time left the house, more than ninety minutes later. Having completed her work the previous week, Witch only needed minutes to check whether the bishop had noticed any alterations to the ledgers. Satisfied that he hadn't, she let herself out without being seen and headed to town where she posted the letters in the box at the main post office, ensuring they'd be on their way first thing the following morning. Having carried out some of her own research she was delighted to discover that Ruben had been a choir boy when younger. This fitted perfectly and all she had to do now was to scare him into carrying out his part of the plan. She smiled to herself, anticipating the enjoyment this would give her.

Too many other students would see her speaking to Ruben if she was to talk to him at school, so this time she opted for catching him on his own as he made his way home. She followed him home one night, careful not to be seen, so knew exactly where he would say goodbye to the two friends he walked with. She appeared at the corner of the next street.

'Hello, Ruben.' She was pleased to see him jump in surprise. 'Sorry, did I scare you?'

'No. Look, I've done everything you asked of me, can't you just leave me alone now?'

'Fancy a milkshake, Ruben?'

'With you? You are kidding, right?'

'Now, now, Ruben. That's not very friendly or polite is it? I know your parents brought you up to be a nice Catholic boy, didn't they?'

'What do you want?'

'Well, Ruben, what I want from you is another small favour and it involves that nice bishop at your church…' And she laid out her plan for him.'

'No way. I'm not doing anything else for you,' he said.

'Well, we can do it the easy way, Ruben, or the hard way. How do you think your parents or the police would feel if I told them you attacked me and tried to force yourself on me?'

'Everyone knows you're crazy and nobody would believe you.'

But Witch could see she had him worried and had sowed the seeds of doubt. 'Well, we'll just have to see who *everyone* believes then, won't we, Ruben? Of course, I don't mind having a few bruises, so it looks authentic.' She lifted her top and showed him the marks she'd already inflicted on Christina. 'They're not the only ones, but we're in the street and it wouldn't be proper to…'

'You're off your head! I'm having nothing to do with your evil…'

'See that couple across the road, Ruben?'

He shook his head, exasperated by her interruption, but looked anyway.

'No, and what's that…'

'Good.' She moved closer to him, smiled, and started to yell, 'Arrgh! Get off me!'

79

She shouted loud enough for the couple to look in their direction, and she ramped up her complaint. 'No, don't hurt me…'

The couple hurried across the road towards them. 'What's it going to be, Ruben?' she whispered, as they approached.

Ruben was starting to sweat but determined not to let her blackmail him into something he knew he shouldn't do. He already regretted snitching on the bishop and his head teacher.

'Are you all right, love?' the woman asked.

She looked at Ruben before answering. His expression showed he wasn't going to budge, yet.

'It's…it's this boy,' she said, spluttering the words out through tears. 'He won't leave me alone and…and… I thought he was going to…'

'I think we'd better call the police and see what they have to say about this,' the man said.

'I didn't do anything…'

'We'll let the police decide that,' the woman said, looking at him like he was pond life.

Ruben looked at each of them in turn, realising that he would have believed her had he been a stranger. Panicking, he took off in the opposite direction of his house, like a zebra being chased by a pride of lions.

'Thank you so much for saving me. I just want to get home now.'

'You've had a shock. We'll take you,' the woman said, but Christina had already left.

'Can I have a word?' Ruben asked in school the following day. He looked worried, like he needed a good night's sleep, which pleased Witch. She could also see he was trying to be discreet and although there weren't many other students by the lockers, those that were there were looking at them.

80

'Same place as yesterday,' she said before walking away.

They discussed how Ruben would drop his bombshell; Witch knew there was no evidence, and this was just another way to sow the seeds of doubt and discredit the bishop. Ruben was now fully on side. He knew it was either his reputation or the bishop's.

The following day at school he approached Miss Zoe, the teacher with whom he had the best rapport and who he felt would believe him.

It was the last class of the day and he hung back until just the two of them were left in the classroom. 'I need to talk to someone, Miss Zoe, before I go out of my mind.'

'Sit down, Ruben. Can you tell me what's wrong?'

'It's something that happened years ago, before my tenth birthday. I thought I'd put it out of my mind but now it's coming back to haunt me and I don't know what to do.'

She could see the worry on his face and placed a hand on his arm. 'You can talk to me about it if you want or I'll arrange for you to see the School Counsellor, or both. We're here to help.'

'The bishop sexually assaulted me,' he blurted out. 'There were only four of us in the church, and I went to the storerooms in the next building when the priest asked me to sort out the candles. The bishop came in and...'

'Oh, you poor boy,' she said, leaning forward. She went to put a hand on his, to comfort him, then thought better of it.

'You don't believe me,' he said. 'When he did it he said nobody would believe me and that I'd go to hell if I said anything. And that's why I haven't told anyone.'

81

'Of course I believe you, Ruben. We need to report this to get you justice and so that no others are in danger from the bishop.'

'I'm not sure, Miss Zoe. Can I speak to the counsellor first and then decide what to do?'

'Of course. I'll make the appointment and let you know the details tomorrow. We'll talk again at break time tomorrow morning. But, Ruben, I'm duty bound to speak to the head about this so she can inform the authorities.'

'Do you have to?'

'I do, yes. Now that you've told me we must get you the help you need, and... what's that mark on your arm?' she asked, noticing the cigarette burn for the first time.

Ruben said nothing but looked down and his teacher put two and two together and came up with the wrong conclusion.

'This makes it even more important for you to see someone right away. You need help to stop harming yourself, Ruben, and we must also ensure that nobody else goes through the pain you've endured.'

Ruben nodded, but looked terrified.

'It's going to be all right, Ruben.' This time she did put a reassuring hand on his forearm. 'I can't imagine how awful this is for you, but you will get through this.'

'Thanks, Miss Zoe. But please don't tell anyone else for now. I need to speak to my parents and they love the church.'

'You don't have to do this on your own, Ruben. One of us can be with you when you tell your parents if you prefer? Why don't we get you an appointment with the counsellor first and you can talk to him about it? Unless you want to tell your parents this evening? I'll ask him for an appointment tomorrow.'

'It can wait. I'd prefer someone to be with me,' Ruben said, knowing that if he was going to ruin someone's life, he'd rather have company while he was doing it - he might break if his parents asked too many questions. And he didn't want to imagine the consequences from that evil bitch, Christina. He had contemplated going against her wishes and taking the flack, but the thought of that was horrendous and this was definitely the lesser of the two evils.

'Are you all right to go home now or do you want me to come with you?'

'I'll be all right thanks, Miss Zoe.'

'Here's my phone number, Ruben…' She wrote it down on a piece of paper and handed it to him. 'Now that you've decided to do something about this, it may bring back more vivid memories. Call me at any time if you need to talk.'

'The memories can't get any more vivid than they already are, but thanks anyway.'

He left the room and she watched him go. The church had a lot to answer for, but Zoe knew she had her work cut out convincing the head who adored and respected the bishop. Maria, the secretary, had already left so Zoe knocked and entered on the command.

The head carried on writing without looking up while Zoe stood waiting. She couldn't be bothered with the mind games today so spoke without worrying about interrupting the head's concentration.

'I have an urgent matter to discuss, Mrs…'

'So I see.' The head put down her pen and looked up. 'Sit down, Zoe.' She didn't add *this had better be good*, but Zoe could see from her expression that she wasn't happy.

'Ruben Groot stayed behind after class today. He was very distressed…' She hesitated for a few seconds and noticed that the head's demeanour had changed, and she now had her full attention.

'Go on, Zoe, what is it?'

'Ruben told me that he was sexually abused by the bishop just before his tenth birthday.'

'How preposterous and absolute piffle! I know the bishop very well and he's not capable of that sort of behaviour, whereas Ruben. Well he's...'

'He's a very distressed young man who needs counselling. He's also been self-harming and I'm extremely worried. I know it's a shock and not easy to hear, but I believe him, and this has to be investigated at the very least. I'm going to contact the counsellor as soon as I leave your office and arrange an emergency appointment, but you needed to know about this first.'

'Yes, you're right, Zoe.' She tapped her pen on the desk, the only sound in the room as she thought about what she'd been told. Zoe waited patiently. 'If he decides to go ahead with this complaint, we'll have to inform the police and it'll be investigated. It'll ruin the bishop's career and bring the church into disrepute.'

'And it'll also stop other boys from being abused. And if we can...'

'I know the bishop well and he's not the type to...'

'Well enough to know what goes on behind closed doors, Mrs Windt?'

The head gave Zoe a warning look which she decided to ignore. 'With all due respect, if the school doesn't report it to the police it could ruin our reputation, not to mention what harm it might cause Ruben in the future. And if something happens to another boy later down the line...'

'Don't you *all due respect* me, Miss Hoek! I'm well able to work out the consequences if this is not reported.'

It was the first time in ages that the head had used her family name and spoken to her in such a manner and Zoe was furious. 'In that case, Mrs Windt,

84

I'll leave you to it and I'll go and make the appointment for Ruben. Being the boy's mentor, I trust I'll be included in any decisions that are going to affect Ruben while he's in school?' She didn't wait for an answer as she left the office and closed the door behind her.

Zoe went home and poured herself a large glass of wine some thirty minutes later. The counsellor had been very flexible, and the appointment was arranged for ten o'clock the following morning.

The scandal reached the national news and the bishop knew his career was over. The Archbishop was willing to stand out on a limb for him about the alleged sexual assault, believing the bishop when he said he had never touched anyone inappropriately in his whole life, but when it came to theft and fraud he decided to err on the side of caution and ignore any misgivings he had on the matters. The irony that everything was ruined due to financial impropriety rather than sexual activity wasn't lost on the bishop as the police read the charges out to him. He was disgraced, defrocked, and disillusioned as the judge sentenced him to five years in prison – making an example of him because he refused to plead guilty and professed his innocence until they took him down.

He knew it was all the doing of the girl, and on the worst days he prayed for forgiveness for what he would like to do to the evil spirit her body was host to. The bishop was still determined to rid the host of the demon and vowed to make it his life's work once he left the prison. In the meantime, he'd heard a prisoner wanted him to know what it was like when the shoe was on the other foot, and the bishop's gut tightened in knots as the guards disappeared from the corridor and the big man entered his cell along with two of his cronies. As they held him down and the leader did his worst, the ex-bishop prayed hard for the souls of all three.

*****

With the bishop off the scene, Christina knew she could make plans for her future. Despite, or perhaps because of her demon, she knew she'd have to make her own way in life with little to no help from others. She studied hard, knowing that she needed to be financially independent as soon as she could be. She left school aged eighteen and the local council found her a room in a halfway house where she could prepare for adulthood, with the help of support workers. The managers, a husband and wife named Mr and Mrs de Jong, lived in the home.

Totally self-sufficient, she worked hard during the times Witch left her alone, trying to learn practical skills that would enable her to cope with life and give her a career that would make her enough money to live without the help of others. She'd been good with numbers throughout school, so decided on accountancy and enrolled on a course in the local college. Witch's voice often told her that it was a boring choice.

'I have to be financially independent and it's the only thing I'm good at,' was Christina's standard reply.

'I'll teach you how to be good at other things,' Witch informed her, 'then you won't have to work hard.'

She knew none of these *things* would be good so tried to suppress the urges when Witch wanted to take over. Even though the demon always won out, Christina was stubborn enough to keep trying, and on these occasions she had to excuse herself from studies due to her severe headaches.

Mrs de Jong was very supportive for the first six months and Christina came to think of her as a wise aunt-like figure. She was taught how to cook, clean and to manage her finances, though already proficient in the latter.

86

As usual, Witch ruined it for her and when Mrs de Jong found Christina and her husband in a compromising position, she lost the plot.

'This is how you repay everything?'

'But it was the voice inside my head. She takes over my body and I can't do anything about it. You don't understand,' Christina cried. 'Nobody understands.'

'Pack your bags, you're leaving,' Mrs de Jong said. 'And you,' she added to her husband, 'we're through.'

He knew his wife well enough to know she would never forgive him and was sad his marriage had ended this way, but now he had a beautiful, new, young, plaything.

'I'm sorry. But it was bound to happen,' he said. 'I'll find somewhere for me and Christina and will arrange a time to collect my stuff.'

'You and me?' Witch said. 'You don't really think so do you?' She looked Mr de Jong up and down, very slowly. 'Seriously?' she asked, bursting into gales of laughter.

The adults looked at her as if she were mad. 'So, you just toyed with my husband because you felt like it?'

If she noticed the girl's conflicting emotions, Mrs de Jong decided to ignore them. 'Just go, Christina.'

The pattern repeated itself for the next two years during her studies, but the authorities bailed her out as often as they could, though her support worker despaired. There were a number of sighs of relief when Christina qualified, and social services acknowledged there was nothing further they could do for the young woman. A support network was in place to continue helping young adults who were transitioning to total independence. Christina would have been happy to have the safety net to fall back on, but Witch wanted none of it.

It didn't take her long to find her place in the belly of the city. People she came into contact with soon realised the beautiful girl could be crazy as hell, and when she lost her temper, she didn't seem to mind if she hurt herself as well as others. Witch thrived in the city and earned enough money through theft and prostitution to find a small place of her own. She was in charge of her own destiny, and when powerful men wanted more from her, she cleverly manipulated them into doing whatever she needed, without them even realising. She revelled in her physical beauty and used it to get exactly what she wanted.

Christina was relieved that she didn't know everything that Witch had done, but struggled with the guilt of what she did know.

'You're weak and pathetic,' her demon told her often, and Christina fought with her less and less, unable to tolerate the unbearable pounding in her head.

When the head of a private bank wanted some arm candy, Christina agreed to work for him in the hope of some normalcy in her life. When his wife discovered the affair and threatened divorce, he ended their relationship. It was the first time in her adult life that a man had broken up with her. Witch was furious and Christina was bemused when he asked her to sign some papers.

'This is a non-disclosure agreement,' he said. 'And this should keep you in the lifestyle to which you've become accustomed, so you don't need to work unless you really want to.' He handed her the cheque. 'It's been fun.'

Her smile belied her true feelings and Witch added his name to the list of people she wanted to destroy. Craving routine, Christina found a job in the finance department of a retail company, hoping to work her way up. It wasn't the life Witch wanted for them both and she missed the excitement.

She was drinking a coffee and people-watching one day, pondering on how to destroy her former lover, when a good-looking dark-haired man approached.

'Mind if I join you?' he asked in English that held a hint of a sexy French accent. Witch put all thoughts of past wrongs on hold for the moment as she decided to have some fun with the new man.

It was the beginning of a relationship that would give her the excitement she hankered after and take her to the highlands of Scotland and a meeting with a very interesting twin.

Chapter 5 – The Highlands

Scottish Northern Nature, the charity responsible for the upkeep of a large number of heritage sites and nature reserves in the Scottish Highlands, was in trouble.

'It's a combination of the virus and the wildcats,' Ian McDonald, the head of the charity told the Committee during the crucial meeting to decide the way forward. His expression was as grumpy as that of the supersized tabby cats they were trying to save from extinction.

The murmurs around the table signified concern and agreement. The worldwide virus had made potential visitors nervous about travelling, even though immunisation was now available by way of a new vaccine to combat the disease. They'd lost funds from tourism and some of the businesses who made regular donations to the charity had gone bust, meaning that the donations had dried up. It was a perfect storm and the situation was dire.

'At least the cat population is growing,' Margaret Cameron said. 'So we've managed to save a species. For now, anyway.

Ian acknowledged that the wildcat population had almost doubled to two hundred. 'But without money from visitors we won't be able to continue the programme,' he said. 'And we'll be back where we started in a few years.'

The murmuring began again. Ian had set the scene and now had to make them think it was their idea. He had a way to go yet.

'I'm after ideas to raise funds. Please look at the minutes in front of you from the last meeting. We've incorporated suggestions at Point 5,' he said, stopping to give those around the table a chance to look. 'I want fresh, innovative suggestions or ideas. We've all had three months to think about this…'

After an initial silence, William Young looked at Ian and the other committee members. He coughed to clear his throat. 'This may be controversial, but I've wracked my brains trying to think of a way to get out of this financial mess and to preserve as many heritage and nature sites as we can. My only conclusion is that we have to sell some land. Short-term pain for long-term gain…'

'No!' said Margaret, knowing that William was Ian's sound-piece. If we sell the land we've lost it for ever and_'

'Margaret,' Ian interrupted, turning to the committee who were all talking over each other. 'Please, ladies and gentlemen, let me explain. There aren't going to be any easy decisions today…' He looked pointedly at Margaret. 'We have to raise enough funds to get by for the next few years until tourism gets back to normal levels. We can't start any new projects and can only hope to stop sites and buildings from further degradation. I'm open to all suggestions.'

Knowing that they'd explored all other options barring the sale of land, Ian waited.

'As there are no further ideas,' said William, 'I'd like to propose that we sell our land in Glenmalvern to the highest bidder.'

'I second this proposal,' said another of Ian's yes men.

'All in favour?' asked Ian and nodded for the Secretary to count the number of hands.

'Against?'

Margaret raised her hand and gave her two supporters who raised theirs a grateful look. They were too few and knew they'd lost the battle.

'Proposal carried,' said Ian. 'We'll place the advertisement next week and call a meeting as soon as we have some interest.'

He knew that would be in no time at all as he already had a buyer lined up.

*****

Andrew Robertson sat in the back of his Range Rover, his mother in the seat next to him, on the way to visit his brother, Sandy.

'I'm fed up with all of this travelling, Andrew.'

'Me too, Mum. But you know the situation.'

She ignored his comment. 'We have to take this horrendous journey every three months, Andrew, when there's a facility Alexander could be transferred to just a stone's throw from our own front door. Why can't you do something about it, Son? I thought you were a man of influence?' The last was said in a mocking tone and Andrew leaned forward to close the reinforced plastic screen behind his driver, in the hope he wouldn't be able to hear the full conversation.

'I've told you, Mum, I've tried. The authorities say they can't transfer Sandy just now, but they'll let us know when_'

'That's what you said last time, and the time before, Son. They can't still be full up, surely?'

'Apparently there's no more space for the criminally insane in Scotland, so we'll have to keep doing this journey. And I heard that_'

'Alexander isn't criminally insane, Andrew. He's not well that's all. If that wife of his hadn't cheated on him they'd still be_'

Here we go, thought Andrew, as he acknowledged that his mother was still totally in denial about his brother's brutal murder of his wife when he discovered she'd had an affair.

'You do remember that Sandy cheated on Heather first and they were going to be divorced anyway?'

'She was no good, that woman. Drove him to do what he did, I tell you. Brought disgrace on the family, that wicked woman. I remember when Alexander was a child…'

And here we go again, thought Andrew for the second time that minute. He had long since come to terms with the fact his mother blamed anyone but his brother for his shortcomings, mistakes, and later in life, his crimes. They'd been doing this journey for nearly three years now, since his brother had been transferred from a mainstream prison in Glasgow after murdering one prisoner and deforming another. Yet their mother was in total denial, always insisting it was somebody else's fault, just as she had when the brothers were children when Andrew always got blamed for his younger brother's misdemeanours. As they grew, the misdemeanours turned from pranks against him and other kids, to bullying and violence.

From a young age, Sandy had been a cruel kid. Andrew recalled stopping him tying bangers to a cat's tail one November near bonfire night. He felt nothing but contempt for him and was glad he was locked up for life but his own life would have been easier had the authorities approved the move to the facility in the Highlands, and it had taken him a while to discover why this move hadn't been possible. It wasn't going to happen now, and Andrew had come to terms with this. But he hadn't come to terms with the fact that he'd been hoodwinked for almost three years. They didn't know who they were messing with - but they would find out, soon enough.

'…Are you listening to me, Son?'

'Of course I am, Mum, yes. You were saying what a good boy Sandy was, before Dad's accident, and how everything changed because of *that woman.*'

'That's right, Andrew. At least Michele's given you a son and me a wonderful grandson. Heather couldn't even do that.'

The best his mother could say of his own wife was that she'd given them Andre. He knew his mother wasn't a fan of Michele, but they'd had words years before and he'd made it perfectly clear that if she decided to travel down that road it would be bumpy at best, and at worst, there'd be no going back. Both mother and son had accepted this impasse and when she realised the sort of woman his mother was, his French wife was more than happy to take her husband's advice and to keep her distance as much as she could.

Andrew waited for a natural break in his mother's ramblings so he could give her the news.

'I have news about the prison hospital at Glenmalvern, Mum.' He didn't give it the correct title, knowing his mother would only kick off again if he used the phrase *criminally insane.* 'They're going to close it within the next six months and transfer all the inmates, sorry, patients, down South. So please think again about this journey in future and consider taking flights. I'll still come with you, of course, and it'll be much easier for you than having to sit in a car for nigh on ten hours.' *Not to mention for me having to put up with all the stories about what a wonderful son Sandy was.*

'You know I hate flying,' she replied, fidgeting in her seat. 'Having to breathe the same air as all those people spreading their germs. Yuck! And you know I like looking at the countryside.'

'How about the train, Mum? First Class, of course, and you'd still be able to see the countryside flying by.'

'I'm definitely not flying, Son, and I'll think about the train.

'Good, you do that,' he said, knowing he'd have the same conversation the next time and the time after and wondering how long before his mother drove him totally nuts.

'Now, how's that wee boy of ours? He's so like his Uncle Alexander,' his mother said, moving on to her second favourite subject after Sandy. The wee boy was Andre, Andrew and Michele's twenty-five-year-old son who worked for Highland Eco Enterprises, the Scottish part of the family business. Andrew had tried to knock any likeness to his own brother out of his son when he was a youngster. He believed he'd done a good job, and so far, and the *wee boy* hadn't displayed any of his uncle's criminal tendencies. His girlfriend could be unpredictable at times, but she was a beauty. Andrew smiled to himself, proud that his son had attracted such a beautiful woman; in that respect he was his father's boy. He'd trained him well and had a job for Andre that would test his son's abilities and, he hoped, expose the liars at the so-called prison hospital. If he could disgrace Sir Paul Field and his cronies, all the better. If all went to plan, it would also give the family business ample opportunity to acquire some new land at a bargain price.

Chapter 6 – Andre and Christina

Andre jumped out of bed as the phone rang, not wanting to wake his beautiful girlfriend lying next to him.

'How are you both, Son?'

'All good here,' he lied, having no intention of telling his father that the honeymoon period was over and there were layers to Christina he had not suspected.

'I have a job for you, Andre, and it might need a woman's touch. I want to discuss it with you in person and was planning on coming to Amsterdam. I know you probably don't want to spend a whole weekend away from Christina, but if you can fit me in, we can make a weekend of it if you like?'

'I can do that, Dad. It'll make Christina want me all the more when I get back,' Andre said, knowing better than to bite the hand that fed him and telling his father exactly what he wanted to hear.

'That's my boy!' Andrew laughed. 'I'll email you the details when Cathy's booked everything.'

Andre returned to the bed and lay down, looking at the woman he'd thought he knew. She was like an addiction, but the previous night's passion had been a massive jump beyond what they usually did. He inspected the scratches on his thighs, still red raw from her nails. And wondered what would have happened if he hadn't calmed her down before her hands were further up his body. Andre shuddered involuntarily. Despite the pain, he'd nearly exploded from the excitement and thinking about it now gave him a huge erection.

He lay down, spooning Christina so she felt his hardness, and began fondling her breasts. As soon as she turned around and smiled, he was relieved to see his good girl was back.

'Morning, handsome,' she said, kissing him.

Andre was thankful as she caressed him gently, and they snuggled up to each other sometime later, once their lovemaking was over.

'I don't know what was in your wine last night,' he said, 'but I think you should give it a miss for a while, until my skin heals.'

'Whatever you say, my darling. Coffee and french toast?'

'Perfect, thanks.'

All is well and she knows her place, he thought, watching her leave the bedroom. *…and maybe a bit of occasional rough sex in future will keep it fresh and exciting.* He put any further doubts out of his mind as he took a shower and prepared for the work day ahead.

*****

Andre left their apartment on the outskirts of the city and took a train to the centre. He checked in to the Waldorf Astoria, the stunning, top of the range hotel in the heart of Amsterdam, and only twenty kilometres from Schiphol International Airport which his father was flying into. He waited in the bar as pre-arranged.

'Hello, Son,' his father called, after he had checked in.

'Hi, Pa.' It was past midnight, but Andre had waited up for him.

Andrew shook hands with his son then squeezed him in a bear hug. They hadn't seen each other in over a month and when the hug was over, Andrew kept hold of his son's upper arms and looked him in the eyes. 'How are you, Andre?'

'Life's good, Pa. Working hard and playing hard, too, but not so much now I have Christina.'

Andrew's laugh boomed out in the quiet bar and he didn't notice the irritated looks of a few of the

97

patrons. 'That's what I want to hear,' he said. 'Let's get a seat and have a quick catch up.'

As always, Andre followed his father's lead without giving it a second thought. 'How's Maman since I saw her in Paris the other week?'

'Your mother's fine, Andre. That reminds me, she sends her love and is looking forward to seeing you and Christina again. I told her you'd be busy if you take on the new project I have for you, but we'll get together after that. Your grandmother sends her love, too, and was whinging that she doesn't hear from you often enough.'

'I'll call her next week. The new project, Pa? What does that involve?'

'I thought we'd take in the delights of the city tomorrow and Sunday, then we'll discuss the business and the project on Sunday night, so you can sleep on it and make your decision on Monday morning before we leave.'

'My decision? But you know if you want me to do something I'll always say yes. It won't be a problem.'

Andrew swelled with pride and reminded himself that his son was one in a million. He might take after his Uncle Sandy in looks, but thankfully, that's where it ended; he was nothing like him in manner or personality.

'I do know that, Andre, and I'm lucky that we can trust each other one hundred percent. You don't yet know how important that is in business.'

'I think I do.'

'Okay, so maybe you do. But the project I have for you is not without risk and you have the choice to accept or decline. I won't think any better or worse of you, whichever you decide.'

They both knew Andre would accept the project, whatever it was, but Andre appreciated his father giving him the choice, and he was intrigued at what was going to be asked of him, hoping it was more exciting than his current, mostly office-based, role.

'Enough for now. I'm going to finish my drink and get off to bed. What about you, Son?'

It was the first time that his father had given him a choice instead of suggesting he do the same too, and Andre was pleasantly surprised.

'I'm going to have another quick drink before calling it a night,' he said, but only because he was curious to test the waters.

'We'll meet for breakfast at 8.30, give us plenty of time for a full day in the city. Goodnight, Andre.'

'Goodnight, Pa. Sleep well,' Andre said, hoping that this was the start of his father truly treating him like an adult. He drank his beer quickly and retired fifteen minutes after his father, not anticipating either of the surprises that were in store for him that weekend.

'Anything you want to do today, Andre?' Andrew asked over breakfast the following morning. Andre and Christina rarely came into the city; she preferred visiting other places whenever Andre had a free weekend, so he took the opportunity to play the tourist.

'I was thinking maybe a canal trip to take in the city's architecture or perhaps the Rijksmuseum?' He knew his father was into his art and had copies of Rembrandt and Vermeer's work in their country house in the Highlands.

'Good choice. I'm up for both. Do you want to see the Anne Frank House?'

'Not bothered about that, Pa, but I would like to buy a piece of jewellery for Christina, and, er…' He hesitated, but then decided to go for it. 'De Wallen, the red-light district. I might want to sample a few of the delights on offer there.'

'That's my boy,' Andrew answered, in a fairly good impression of Spike, the Tom and Jerry cartoon bulldog.

The novelty of the day wasn't lost on Andre as they did most of the things he wanted without his father complaining or suggesting anything different. Running out of time later that day, they decided to leave the canal trip until Sunday.

He hadn't told his father the reason for wanting to spend time with one of the prostitutes in the red-light district. It was enough for him to know he was going to do it and both father and son had a silent understanding that they wouldn't discuss it with his mother or girlfriend. Andre couldn't complain about his father cheating on his mother when he was cheating on the girl he planned to eventually marry, now they'd cleared up the rough sex business. His parents showed each other respect, and he thought they loved each other as they had been together for almost thirty years. His father worked long hours and his mother often spent time at their home in the French countryside when his father was too busy to slacken off during weekends. He'd grown Eco Enterprises from scratch, and it gave the family luxuries that most could only dream of. Andre didn't mind working hard to reap the rewards, and he had done so as soon as his education had finished.

At De Wallen district that night, Andre discovered that there were few Dutch good time girls and most of those offering their services were foreign. The one he chose was a short, dark-haired girl with curves in all the right places. They negotiated a price of one hundred and fifty euros for one hour. Her room was small and brightly coloured and was exactly as he imagined a room in this area would look like. But it was clean, and comfortable enough for his needs.

'Take off your clothes,' she said, all business-like.

Andre took another one hundred and fifty euros out of his wallet. 'Can we negotiate extras first?' he said, waving the money in front of her.

'You're the boss,' she replied, and Andre told her what he wanted.

Just less than an hour later, he asked if she had a shower and she showed him to it. Nothing was missing when he returned to the room and they said their goodbyes.

'You know where to find me if you come back to Amsterdam,' she said, keen for him to remember her so she could make some more easy money. 'Goodbye, Andre.'

Andre had arranged to meet his father at the Central Station; a ten-minute walk from the red-light district. On the walk there, he wondered why rough sex with a prostitute was both less painful and satisfying than that with his girlfriend. This wasn't the first prostitute he'd been with – the two other times had been on dares after drunken nights out with friends, and he hadn't remembered much about them - but he was now certain that he'd never go out for sausages again when he could have his fill of steak at home.

The décor of the restaurant his father had picked was upmarket and classy, in stark contrast to where both men had been less than an hour earlier. The streets were buzzing as they left the restaurant and shortly after, Andre followed his father into an Irish bar where live music was playing.

'Two pints of lager,' Andrew shouted to be heard at the busy bar, and further conversation between father and son was impossible, so they listened to the live music and took in the atmosphere.

After a lazy breakfast on Sunday, the men took a canal trip, visited the Van Gogh Museum, and later, had a walk around Vondelpark,

'It's named after the famous Dutch poet whose statue graced the park,' Andrew informed his son.

It was a sunny but cool day, and the park was very busy. Andre was keen to hear about the project his father wanted him to carry out, but resisted raising the subject, knowing his father would tell him in his own good time.

That evening, Andrew managed to get a table next to the window, with a view of the beautifully manicured gardens at the two Michelin starred Spectrum Restaurant in the hotel. Andre opted for Sea Bass while his father decided on blue lobster for the main. Everything about the restaurant was superb, but Andre still had to curb his impatience as he was almost bursting to know what his father had in mind for him.

The sweets finished and coffee served, Andrew smiled at his son. 'I've enjoyed these few days, Andre. We don't do it often enough.'

'Me too, Pa.'

'But now to business. Firstly, let's talk about Sir Paul Field. I've kept this to myself, son, but a number of us were in the running to acquire land in central London, to build on. It came down to the two of us, but unfortunately for me, his bid won.'

'Why didn't you tell me?'

'The only people who knew, Andre, were key members of my legal and finance team. I didn't tell you or your mother as I was convinced I'd win this time, and I wanted to surprise you both. Sadly, it wasn't meant to be.'

The look on his father's face told Andre he was more than sad. 'You said *this time*, Pa. What else has happened?'

'Years ago when I wanted to buy some land in the Highlands near Glenmalvern, he outbid me, and I lost that too. Arbuthnot and Lee are above Eco Enterprises in the top one hundred companies, and it seems to me that whenever an opportunity arises for me to achieve my dreams, that bastard always pips me to the post.'

Andre's father hadn't opened up to him before, and he was surprised to see this vulnerable side of him. Realising he was human after all, he listened as his father continued to list the times when Sir Paul Field had managed to win contracts, or achieve something that had been elusive to his father or the company.

'Three years ago, I had a tip off that I could expect a knighthood in the Queen's New Year's Honours. I'm so glad I didn't tell you and your mum about that one, Andre, and you can only imagine how I felt when it was announced that Paul Field had been knighted and I hadn't.'

'I had no idea, Pa. Sorry.'

'It's fine, son, I'm over it now. But I've been doing some digging. I've always wondered why he never developed the Glenmalvern land. I had rough plans for a ski resort and…'

'But that's where the facility for the criminally insane is? Why would anyone develop the land around that area?'

'That was just an old hospital back in the day, son. It's only changed since Paul Field bought the land- and that's something else that doesn't fit. When I tried to get your Uncle Sandy a place there, all I came up against were barriers, despite my contacts in the government. The past years would have been so much easier on your grandmother if she hadn't had to travel down south to visit him.'

'So that's another thing to be annoyed with Sir Paul about?'

103

'It certainly is.' Andrew laughed bitterly. 'It doesn't add up, son. The fact that he didn't develop the land when anyone else would have, and that I can't get a place in the facility for your uncle despite my high-level contacts, raised a few alarms and made me do some digging. I used the Freedom of Information Act to try to find out about the facility and the inmates. When I was met by closed doors, I also used my contacts and a few who would like to see Sir Paul Field knocked down in size; but the funny thing, Andre, is that I've come up against brick walls on all fronts.'

'I see.'

'I don't think you do, Son. This is unprecedented and I smell a rat. A bloody big one at that, and this is where you come in.'

'But if you can't get the information at your level, how can I?'

'There's more than one way to skin a cat, son. Let's talk about the different ways and then decide whether you've got what it takes to see this project through for our family, *and* we'll see whether Sir Paul Field is exactly who and what he says he is.'

*****

Christina had dinner all ready for Andre's return and she looked at the table with satisfaction. She'd paid his favourite restaurant to deliver everything he loved and the table was set for a romantic dinner for two. She left the blinds open and the lights from the beautiful city in the distance shone like stars in a moonlit velvet sky. The chef gave her final instructions for heating the main course, and left, quietly closing the door behind him.

A few minutes later she heard the key in the lock and Andre rushed into the apartment like a tornado, picking Christina up off her feet and swinging her around.

104

'I've missed you, my darling Christina,' he said. Before she had a chance to respond he kissed her as if he'd been away for months, not days.

She smiled seductively when they came up for air. 'I've missed you too, Andre.' She pressed her body into his and was more than happy when she felt the reaction. Dinner forgotten for the moment, without further words they went to the bedroom and made love. Andre knew exactly what to do to bring her to orgasm, unlike all the other times when she'd had to gently guide his hands. Christina was thoughtful when they finished, but smiled at her lover. 'Don't go anywhere,' she said, 'I'll be back.' She closed the bathroom door and leaned against it for a moment.

'You know, don't you?' Witch's voice interrupted her thoughts. It was obvious, even to Christina, that Andre had learnt some new skills while he'd been away. While she appreciated that he wanted to please her, he could have asked instead of visiting a sex worker. Despite her feelings for Andre, she couldn't put up with any form of cheating and knew this was the death knoll for their relationship.

'No!' The voice was loud in her head. 'We have everything we need here. Just get even, it'll be fun. Then leave him.'

'I'm not like...'

'I'll make your life hell if you don't, and you'll end up in prison,' Witch said, and Christina felt the pounding starting, like a drill hammering in her head.

'But so will you and what will that achieve?' she persevered, trying to reason with the demon.

'Do you want me to show you?'

Christina didn't and knew she'd lost for the time being. The Witch took over for the rest of the night, allowing Christina back only occasionally.

'What a night,' Andre said, as they finished their chocolate mousse and Christina began serving liqueur coffees. He caught hold of her wrist and, keeping his eyes locked with hers, fished a long, narrow box from his pocket and passed it to her, saying, 'I love you, Christina. I hope you like it.'

The bracelet was exquisite. Yellow, white and rose gold, it had tiny diamonds separating each gold section and was the most beautiful piece of jewellery she'd ever seen.

'It's beautiful and I love it,' she said, her face lighting up with joy as he fastened the clasp on her wrist.

'Glad we haven't left him yet?' asked the voice in her head, and she silently told her to shut up.

When they went to bed later, Andre fell asleep straight away, having no idea of Christina's true feelings.

Christina laid awake for a while, Witch's voice in her head plotting the revenge against her lover. Eventually the voice stopped and Christina was able to go to the one place where the evil woman hadn't invaded her mind. Yet.

She woke to the sound of voices and the smell of coffee, eggs and bacon. Andre didn't cook, so she rightly assumed he'd had breakfast delivered. The fact that he was trying to please her didn't take away the hurt of knowing he'd slept with another woman. Deceit was deceit, even if he had paid for the services.

'Shut up and smile,' said Witch. Christina didn't want to end up on the street or worse, so knew she'd do just that, at least for now.

By the time she got out of the shower there were no voices coming from the kitchen so she brushed her hair, dressed in her lounge wear and went to say good morning.

'Someone's been busy.'

'Good morning, darling,' he replied, giving her a kiss. 'I made the coffee and this,' he swung his arm indicating the food on the table, 'is from the deli. Made this morning and just delivered. Water and coffee?' he asked, pouring both before they sat down to eat. 'My father's given me a job, Christina, and I'm going to need some help. It's nothing to do with accounting.'

'Well that's a relief,' Witch said, inside her head.

'Tell me more.' Christina was genuinely interested and she picked up her coffee and prepared to listen.

'It's not strictly kosher and we could get into trouble if we get caught.'

'Well, we'll have to make sure we don't get caught then,' said Witch who'd taken over, loving the sound of the new job, even though she had no idea what it involved.

'There's a building in Scotland that my father thinks isn't what it seems. He wants us to discover its real purpose, get the information into the media and discredit the man who owns the land the building is on. He believes the land is coming up for sale and he wants to buy it, under a different name and company.'

'Wow! That's going to take some doing. We'll need help.'

'Spot on, Christina. That's your first job. I want you to recruit some people to help us, and whoever you pick, if the worst happens my father's name has to be kept out of it. Nothing can be traced back to him.'

'But what about us?' she asked, raising her eyebrows.

Andre rubbed his chin before answering. 'We need to ensure nothing can be traced back to us either, but as we're going to be taking all the risks, I'm being honest when I tell you this may not be possible. I'll understand if you want nothing to do with this, and it won't change anything between us.'

107

'Accountancy isn't always the most exciting of career paths, Andre,' Christina said drily. 'Everything's set up in the office and I can manage my side of things remotely for a while. I'm ready for an adventure, so I'm in.

'Then we're in this together, darling! I'm so glad you said yes!' He kissed her, then was all business again.

'I'll put you in charge of recruiting to start with, then something a little more adventurous. You may want to start…'

'Let me do some research and come up with some suggestions, Andre. Then, if you're not happy, you can guide me in the right direction.'

He agreed and she started trawling some websites via the dark web.

Chapter 7 – The Missions

Christina pulled the sleeve of her jacket over her hand so she didn't have to touch the dirty door handle with her bare flesh. This wasn't the type of establishment she'd become used to since being with Andre, or even prior to that. Ignoring the shabby lobby as much as she could, she queued behind the three people who were waiting to speak to the creepy looking man standing behind the reception desk.

'I'd like to check in,' she said in her best English when it was her turn.

'That's fifty-two pounds, love, including a continental breakfast.'

The receptionist was all business but had an unexpectedly keen eye. He always made sure he appraised the guests, especially the lookers. This one screamed junkie; her eyes were vacant, telling him she was spaced out from something, but it wasn't his job to monitor the customers unless they misbehaved, and she didn't look like trouble. He wondered if she wanted to crash out then go home to her bloke the next day when she recovered from whatever it was she was on. And this one must have a bloke; even looking pale and out of it he could see she was pretty special.

She took the key-card, paid in cash and followed the directions to her room. The place was small, but the room was clean in comparison to the entrance, although it needed a face lift – it was the perfect location when doing a job or observation, but definitely not a place to stay for pleasure.

She lay down, hoping against hope to escape from the madness for a few hours and to recharge her batteries - no such luck.

'Where are we? What are we doing here?' Witch asked.

'Leave me alone. I need to sleep,' she commented into the otherwise empty room, knowing by now that any protest was completely futile.

'Let's explore first, and then find the man.' The voice sounded excited and almost childlike.

Christina got up to use the bathroom. After flushing, she washed her hands then splashed water over her face in an attempt to energise her mind and body. She returned to the room and rummaged in her bag for her hairbrush. Believing she looked reasonably decent under the circumstances, she approached the door.

'We're not going out looking like that,' Witch told her. 'Go and put some make-up on.'

'No, I'm…'

'Behave, Christina. You know what happens if you don't…'

The pain in her head started and she knew if she didn't do as told it would soon become excruciating. She was too tired to fight it.

The receptionist looked at the girl who'd checked in less than twenty minutes earlier, amazed at the transformation. Then, she'd looked out of it, but now she was made up to the nines, had a spring in her step and, from the way she was dressed, was going out to look for a good time. She caught him looking and gave him a sly wink, flicked back her hair and walked out of the door. *Someone will get lucky tonight*, he thought, then frowned, knowing that it wasn't him.

*****

Still in the mysterious world between sleep and wakefulness, Tony put out an arm and felt the coldness of a cotton sheet against his skin which woke him. He nodded off but was awake again not much later. This dozing wakefulness continued for what felt like forever. He had more than come to terms with the fact that his wife had cheated on him before being murdered, but he

110

still missed having someone to hold in the dark of the night and to share the daylight hours with. It had been easier when she'd first died when the shock and anger of what she'd done had got him through the days and nights, but now the anger had left and he could think about things logically, the pain of her deceit still gave him some sleepless nights.

Eventually he checked his fitness tracker watch and the time flashed up - 02.22. He shook his head and went to the bathroom. Claire had been right when she'd said he was drinking too much, but Tony knew that it would take a little while for him to be able to have a good night's sleep without the aid of alcohol. Splashing water in his face made him feel more awake and he cleaned his teeth before returning to the bedroom to get dressed. He decided to go for a walk, hoping that would clear his head. He dressed in jeans and t-shirt, threw on a jacket to protect him from the wind, grabbed his man-bag and left his house.

He should have noticed someone was watching his house at that time in the morning, but he didn't - and he had no idea of the future consequences of his actions.

Walking towards the out of town shopping centre, he was surprised to see lights shining from a supermarket and a DIY shop. Like a beacon in the darkness he headed towards the lights.

There were one or two other customers wandering around aimlessly in the 24-hour DIY shop; people like him, who struggled to sleep he assumed, plus a small group of staff who were chatting in one area and a few others who were stacking shelves, all waiting for the long night to pass, he didn't doubt. He decided his bathroom could do with a lick of paint and bought a tin of duck egg blue paint from the bored-looking checkout assistant. She yawned as she took the money from him, grunted a thanks, and got back to whatever was previously occupying her on her phone. *If she's taken over in the Zombie Apocalypse, nobody would notice,* he thought as he exited the store.

As he walked around the corner to start his journey home, a voice attracted Tony's attention and he turned around.

'Hello, darling, can you help me?'

The voice came from a woman who had what sounded like a Dutch accent

'You won't get any business here,' Tony replied without thinking. 'I should try the…'

'You cheeky…' She stopped and looked at him in disgust. 'How dare you insinuate…'

'Oh, you're not… I mean I thought…'

'I can see exactly what you thought, but you are definitely barking up the wrong tree. I may be dressed rather provocatively, but I am what you might call a damsel in distress.' Witch paused and offered him a sad smile.

She now had Tony's full attention and his protective instinct kicked in. He wanted to help this beautiful woman more than anything else.

'What's happened and how can I help?' he asked, taking off his jacket and offering it to her.

'That's kind, thank you,' she said. The jacket slipped off one of her shoulders and Tony lifted it and placed it over both. He felt something that had long since been dormant and stepped back in surprise. If the woman noticed, she pretended she hadn't.

'I'm a model and I was invited to this country for my big break. The agency said it would be the making of me. I was a bit worried when they said the shoot was at night, but they convinced me all would be well. The campaign is for a vampire series and they wanted to get some shots of the models walking in the woods with the full moon in the background.' She paused for a moment to collect her thoughts and Tony resisted the urge to comfort her. 'Only it wasn't a shoot. I was in the so-called liaison officer's car and when I wouldn't do what he asked we argued, and he stopped here. I had to get out of the car before the worst happened and he drove away. I didn't even get the chance to grab my stuff. So here I am.'

Tony wasn't sure whether he believed her story, but now that he looked at her properly, she did look slightly dishevelled and he was taken aback by just how stunning she was. Bright blue eyes in an oval shaped face with lips that looked so kissable. Her face was framed by long blonde hair and she was almost as tall as he was, with legs that seemed to go on forever. *Probably is Dutch*, he thought, knowing they were the tallest race in Europe, *and she certainly has model looks*.

'Dutch?' his tired mind asked out loud.

As she laughed, what he was sure of was that she fascinated him and he wanted to get to know her more.

Tony got a grip of himself. 'What I meant to say is how can I help you? Is there anyone I can phone to come and get you?'

'I came over especially for this assignment,' she replied. 'I have no idea where I am or how far I am from the cheap hotel I booked into. All the details are in my purse with my phone so I'll just stay here for the night if you think it's safe here?'

'You'll do no such thing,' Tony replied. 'I can put you up on my settee tonight then we'll get you sorted in the morning. Things always look better in the light of day.'

'I'm not sure...' She knew she had him hook line and sinker, but she didn't want to seem too easy. 'I've already had one scare tonight and the agent, or liaison officer, looked like a decent man, the same as you do. How do I know I can trust you?'

113

'I understand, and you don't. So, all I can do is to give you my word that you won't come to any harm while you're with me. The alternative is to stay here and, dressed the way you are, you may leave yourself open to propositions from people who are looking for…No disrespect meant of course, but the way you've had to dress for the role you were playing means…'

'You're right. I either take you up on your offer or ask the police for help and I'm not sure what they could do. So, can I stay at your place and I'll leave as soon as it's light and I can find my hotel?'

'Of course,' Tony replied, 'but it's a twenty-minute walk first. Can you manage that in those shoes? Or we could try to find an all-night taxi but we might have to wait a while?'

'I'll try,' she said, 'but can I hold onto you to keep my balance?' She didn't tell him that she'd stepped out of a taxi a few minutes earlier around the corner and had taken the driver's number for future use.

They both knew that she could have requested help from the staff in the shop, but neither mentioned it. She linked an arm in his and they started the walk to his home. Tony tried to ignore the stirring in his gut, determined to keep to his word.

But it was she who surprised him when they arrived. He unlocked the door and indicated with his arm that she should go in first. 'After you,'

As he followed and removed the keys from the lock, closing the door behind him, she touched the back of his neck. Tony turned to face her and she smiled, leaned forward and kissed him long and hard. He knew he should have resisted but it had been so long since he had kissed anyone. The last person he had kissed passionately was his late wife, Libby, and those memories were buried, only surfacing in his dreams or during the occasional long, sleepless night.

114

He tried to come to his senses when the kiss stopped and stepped back, putting some space between them. 'Whoa, I thought you were worried about me jumping your bones! Here, I'll show you to the settee and get some blankets.'

They walked into the living room and Tony put on the big light, hoping the brightness would kill the mood and any temptation that went with it. He was sadly mistaken; it only served to enhance her beauty and now he realised that as well as having a beautiful face, her body was perfect too.

'I'll put the kettle on,' he said, drawing away so he could collect his thoughts.

'Do you have anything stronger? I've had a shock tonight and I could do with something to settle my nerves and to help me sleep. I don't even know your name - *kind stranger* sounds too corny.' Her attempt at a joke lightened the atmosphere and Tony smiled, feeling a bit more relaxed, although he did wonder how she could appear so vulnerable one minute and ready to throw herself at him the next. *Maybe it was the shock of earlier,* he thought.

'Tony,' he said, 'my name's Tony. And yours?'

'You can call me Tina.'

'Do you like wine, Tina? White or red?'

'Red would be perfect, thanks,' she said, making herself comfortable as Tony busied himself in the kitchen.

By the time he returned to the living room she was sitting on the settee with her long legs crossed. He tried not to look as he imagined how they would feel wrapped around him. *Get a grip man!* he told himself as he smiled and handed her a glass of wine.

'Thank you for your help, Tony.' She clinked his glass. 'I don't know what I would have done without you tonight and I'll always be grateful.' She took a sip of wine then put the glass down. 'We're both adults, Tony,' she said, uncrossing her legs.

'Yes we are,' he replied as she took his hand and put it on her thigh.

'Do you mind if I kiss you again, it felt so good.'

'You're in shock after what happened to you tonight,' he said. 'I have no intention of taking advantage of you, Tina.'

'But would you mind if I take advantage of you, Tony?'

Her lips on his stopped any further conversation and Tony couldn't even use the excuse of drinking too much wine as, some time later, they left the glasses on the table and, already down to their underwear, she followed him upstairs to his bedroom.

He kissed her passionately, her sighs of encouragement feeding his desire. His lips moved to her earlobe and then down to her neck, taking in every tiny detail about her. As he nuzzled her neck he noticed two small, tear-drop shaped, brown marks and briefly wondered how they got there. The small imperfections only served to enhance her beauty further. Tony moved his lips down her body and she moaned her appreciation. They groaned in pleasure as their lovemaking became explosive.

Afterwards, despite trying to stay awake, Tony fell asleep in her arms, exhausted but completely satisfied. A little while later, when she was sure he was in a deep sleep, Witch sneaked out of the room and went downstairs. She worked fast and returned to bed less than ten minutes later.

It was the real Christina who woke up first in the morning with no idea of where she was or who she was lying next to. This hadn't been the first time and she pushed the rising panic back down as she got up and crept out of the room. A few minutes later she was dressed and looking at the coats and jackets on the stand in the hallway. She took the longest, not bothered that it was too big and looked ridiculous, but satisfied that if she did it up, it would cover both her cleavage and short skirt. As quietly as she could, she tiptoed out of the house and closed the door behind her.

She was long gone by the time Tony woke up and wondered if he'd dreamt the whole thing - then he remembered the sex and he leaned back in the bed and smiled a satisfied smile. He wasn't one for one-night stands, but it had been ages since he'd slept with anyone and last night had scratched an itch that had been there for a while.

He suddenly realised there was no noise and it didn't feel like anyone else was in the house. 'Shit,' he said, coming to his senses.

He jumped out of bed and checked the house. Nothing was missing. *Maybe she's embarrassed about what we did*, he wondered, but he knew deep down that she had wanted him, and he had been too weak to turn her down. Whatever her reasoning, he felt great - initially. He made a cup of coffee and sat at the kitchen breakfast bar, smiling at the memory of what happened. She'd been the first since Libby's death thirteen months before, and with her movie star looks and curves, what a first! They both knew it was simply sex, but he still felt a little disappointed that she'd left without even saying goodbye. And would a girl like that really just turn up out of the blue, sleep with him and disappear on her merry way without taking anything but an old coat? Tony's ego reassured him that he still had the ability to attract beautiful women, while the logical side of his brain tried telling him something was off. He tried to put it out of his mind for a few minutes and deliberately thought about work.

Life was set to carry on as usual. Jim and Tony were due to lead a new course the following week, as instructors of potential new recruits at the school, for a period of two months. On its completion, they planned to go their separate ways for the summer holidays – at the insistence of Fiona – but on return would spend time together with their extended family before starting the new term in the autumn. Sometimes they were pulled from courses when something came up, and the Director would send them off on a new mission to investigate. Depending on where they were in the training and the ability of the attendees, either other instructors would take over, or the students would be given assignments to carry out at home. The twins were used to changing plans at short notice and both enjoyed the variety and excitement of the work. They also appreciated the fact that it was all on a *need to know* basis which gave them a legitimate reason not to give the details to Fiona or their mother which, they believed, meant less worry for the women. But Fiona's new job as one of the techies meant that these days she knew more about some of their missions and Jim didn't have to hide so much from her.

As much as Tony tried to look forward, his behaviour the night before had unsettled him. He shook his head and made a decision. The next few months should give him some stability; he would get Spike back from his mother and keep him at home until he had to go away again. The company of his dog, and concentrating on the course, would be more than enough for him, and he knew he'd take better care of himself if he was also looking after Spike.

The ring tone on his mobile broke his reverie.

'Jim,' Tony said, before even looking at the phone. It was still early and a Sunday morning, so he wondered what was up.

'I'm up early so thought you might fancy going for a run? I'll pick you up in ten minutes.'

'I know something's wrong,' Jim said as they headed towards the quiet countryside in the direction of the School for People with Special Abilities, or SAP School as the employees called it. An hour's drive from Tony's home, deep in the Scottish Highlands, the local populace believed it was a prison for the criminally insane and housed those who had carried out the most heinous of crimes. The town was still very quiet but the route near the school was more challenging and the brothers liked to put their fitness and endurance to the test once a week.

'I couldn't sleep last night so went for a walk and ended up there.' Tony pointed to the DIY store as they drove past it. 'Thought I'd get some paint for the kitchen, it's long overdue and…' Tony's voice trailed off as he saw the look on his brother's face.

'Okay, I'm getting there. When I got back outside, I met this woman who was absolutely stunning. Probably the most beautiful woman I've ever seen. One thing led to another, she came home with me and let's just say that I didn't paint the kitchen.' Tony frowned and his brother knew there was more to it.

'That's not like you, Tony. And didn't it seem strange to you that a woman who you say was so beautiful would come to a DIY store in the back of beyond, especially at that hour of the morning? Didn't you find that at all peculiar?'

'Don't be stupid, Jim. You don't have to be ugly to do DIY. And anyway, she was distressed. Actually, she was dressed like a prostitute and I thought she was propositioning me, then she explained that she was here for a modelling assignment but a guy who was driving her to the location tried it on and got too heavy handed. When she turned him down, he stopped the car and tried again. She said she was scared and ran out of the car but left her belongings in there. She needed help, so I offered, and she planned on reporting the incident to the police this morning. I could obviously see she was a looker and when we got back to my place, she said she wanted me. Being a gentleman, how could I refuse?' Tony gave a gave a half laugh that ended abruptly. 'I just wanted...,' His voice trailed off and he was quiet for a few seconds. Jim waited patiently.

'She's the first since Libby and I didn't want anything complicated. I met someone who wanted to spend the night with me without any complications, exactly the same as I did.'

'I take it she didn't leave her number this morning?'

Tony ignored the question and knew it was no good trying to bullshit his brother. They knew each other too well. He sighed. 'She'd gone by the time I woke up. But don't worry, nothing's missing from the house except one of my old coats, and I assumed she doesn't know where I work.'

'So why the misgivings?'

'I don't know. I have a feeling that I just can't shake off.'

'Right, let's trust your gut. We need to do a complete sweep of your house later. Maybe when you pick Spike up from Mum's?'

'Good idea.'

'Come back to ours for breakfast after we finish, then you go and get Spike and I'll meet you at back at yours.'

'Sounds like a plan,' Tony agreed, knowing that if they both turned up at their mother's to collect Spike, she might suspect something wasn't right.

Jim parked up. The sun had started its daily journey and peeped over the top of a rugged hill in the distance, its rays not yet strong enough to melt the snow-topped peak.

'Come on, let's go,' Jim said, knowing a tough workout would make Tony feel much better. No other cars or people were about, and they started their run without further conversation.

Later that morning, Spike pawed Marion before rushing around the room, over to the door, then looking out of the window. Marion gathered Spike's belongings together and wasn't surprised when her son appeared a few minutes later. She opened the door and Spike galloped out to the garden. He greeted Tony as if he hadn't seen him for a year, and when satisfied that he'd been given the attention he deserved, trotted alongside Tony as they entered the house. Following a quick hello to Marion and Basil with promises of a family get together the following weekend, Spike jumped into the boot of the car and they made their way home.

After a bit of a fuss from Jim when they arrived, Tony showed Spike his favourite ragging rope and the dog knew he had a bit of work to do before he could have fun. Tony had tidied up the kitchen and put the dishes in the washer, all except for his visitor's empty wine glass, which stood unwashed on a counter. He called his dog and let him have a good sniff. In addition, Tony asked Spike to sniff the cushion where Tina had been sitting. He shook the rope again then gave his dog the order.

'Find, Spike.'

Spike ran from room to room and started sniffing. They did upstairs first though both thought it unlikely that she would have bugged the bedroom. Jim smirked then raised an eyebrow as the dog spent some time sniffing by the bed before Tony pulled him away.

Spike stopped halfway down the stairs and sat down. Just in case Tony didn't get the message, he lifted a paw, and pawed the stair he was sitting on. Tony couldn't get his hand under the stair carpet so had to lift it slightly to feel his way in. Sure enough, he felt a small, cold object and when he dragged it out it, discovered it was a listening device. Spike ran down the rest of the stairs, and out of the back door, wagging his tail, obviously pretty pleased with himself. Tony followed him with his ragging rope, and they played for a few minutes before Tony said, 'Work, Spike,' and the dog ran back in the house. The second bug was found under the desk in the computer room, at the far corner, and the men found the third and final device inside the standard lamp in the lounge, after Spike had indicated something was there.

Silently, Jim inspected one of the devices, put all three on the table, then walked towards the back door. He switched on Tony's washing machine before walking outside, beckoning with his finger for Tony to follow. He closed the door behind them and walked to the shed at the very bottom of the garden, then began to talk quietly.

'Standard equipment and nothing unusual about these devices. But I'll get Fiona to check one out thoroughly, just in case she can trace their origins.'

'Yeah, that may help,' Tony replied.

'I take it she knows your name and that she purposely targeted you?'

'I told her my name's Tony, but it's fair to assume that she knows more about me, and maybe others. And before you ask, her name's Tina, or that's what she told me.'

'The Director,' started Jim, but stopped when his brother gave him a look.

'For Christ's sake, Jim, I have needs. I wanted a woman without complications and I thought that's what I got. I thought I struck lucky. How was I supposed to know she had ulterior motives, whatever they might be? We haven't had a security breach for ages and nothing like this has happened to any of the school staff in the past. Well not for as long as we've been part of this organisation, anyway. And as soon as she realises that these aren't working anymore, she'll know that we're on to her so it'll be even harder to catch her or any accomplices, if she has any.'

'And that's why we're outside and out of range, and we're going to put two back to where she left them. Just don't say anything that could be useful to the woman…to Tina, or anyone she could be working with. We certainly don't want them to cotton on and it might be that they'll deem this mission a failure, or even come back for more. In the meantime, you need to tell the Director.'

'I know, and that's one conversation that I'm certainly not looking forward to.'

*****

Tony was called to the Director's office during the twenty-minute morning break the following day.

'By the look of you I assume this is serious. I know nobody's died so you're going to have to tell me what the problem is,' the Director said.

'I've messed up.' Tony sighed. 'I brought a woman back to my house on Saturday night and have since discovered she bugged it.'

'I'm going to need all the information you have, Tony. I assume you didn't get her full name?' The latter was said with a twinkle in his eye and he appreciated the fact that the Director was trying to make him feel better. It had the opposite effect and Tony couldn't have felt worse if he was standing in front of his father as a teenager having heard him say, *I'm disappointed in you.*

He told the Director what he'd told Jim. 'Fiona wants to check out one of the bugs this morning, the others are still at home, so she'll only know that one has stopped working…'

'Good thinking. It's not uncommon and hopefully this woman, Tina, won't suspect. Well done, Tony. I'll speak to Fiona shortly.'

123

'It was Jim's quick thinking, not mine.'

'So you made a mistake, Tony, and I'm not very happy. But you haven't tried to hide it and you and your brother have minimised the impact, so stop beating yourself up. Own it and move on. We have a lot going on during the next six months that I can't talk to you about just yet. Carry on with the course for now and I'll get Fiona and the other techies onto this. But when we find out more, you and Jim need to be mission ready so some extra training during your down time is in order, in case you have to go away at short-notice.'

'Anything else?'

Tony said, 'No,' and went to find Jim, to debrief him about the meeting before the end of the break.

The course continued and the only information the twins discovered during the duration of the course was that Fiona and the others were working on it. Jim knew better than to ask his wife for further information, knowing that she took the signing of the Official Secrets Act as seriously as he did, and didn't want to risk losing her job in the organisation.

It was still early on the Sunday following Friday's end of the course and Tony had just returned from a run with Spike when his mobile phone rang. When he saw his brother's ID on the phone he stayed outside.

'The Director needs to speak to us. I'll pick you up in twenty minutes.'

'Good morning to you too. What's all this about?'

'No idea, but I daresay we'll find out shortly. See you in a bit.'

Tony made a quick coffee and took a shower while it cooled. True to his word, Jim arrived precisely twenty minutes later, along with Fiona. It was not yet eight o'clock.

They made their way to the imposing building that was the SAP School. There had been a near security breach a while ago when an over-enthusiastic journalist had tried to expose the organisation for what it really was. The man had been discredited, but since then, the Director had lost confidence and was almost permanently on edge that their work and the purpose of the school would be discovered. Tony wondered if this was the reason for their meeting. He looked at Jim and knew instinctively that his twin was thinking exactly the same. Fiona had grown used to their telepathy and ignored most of the looks between them.

Despite being long-term senior employees now in charge of the psychic and telepaths wing of the school, Tony and Jim were still subjected to the routine checks performed by the security guards at the outer perimeter, as was with Fiona. There was a cursory check at the inner perimeter and, after parking the car, they all keyed their cards into the building.

'Morning, Fiona, gentlemen. Conference room one,' said the man at reception. The last students had left, so he was one of the two personnel on duty inside.

'Who else is here?' asked Jim as they waited for the lift to the third floor.

'Ryan and Janine, Basil, and your mother.'

'Our mother?' the twins responded in unison, just as the lift doors closed so no further conversation could take place.

Their mother, Marion, worked on a temporary basis as a receptionist and fed any concerns or impressions she had about any students to the Directing Staff. She was currently on a leave of absence, so they were surprised to hear she had been called in for the meeting, too.

'I wonder if this is about…' Tony said, and the twins noticed Fiona looking down to avoid eye contact with either of them. They looked at each other, now

125

realising that something must have happened as a result of the investigation into Tina. They all remained silent until the lift stopped, and they walked along the corridor to the venue.

'In your own time, you three,' The Director's smooth but commanding tone reminded them why they were there, and they entered the room.

They were greeted by all present and told to grab a coffee and take a seat.

At a nod from the Director, Janine pressed a button and the screen on the wall sprung to life.

'Memorise these faces,' said Violet, the Director's wife. 'As a result of Tony's Intel, we've discovered they've been sniffing around the Internet in an attempt to get more information about us.'

The techie geeks monitored any snooping about the school, which included a number of monthly hits from regular members of the public who were naturally curious. The only ones passed to the school executives, currently the members in the room and their spouses, were those who persistently tried to garner further information and were likely to be considered a security risk. This was usually a maximum of one or two per year.

'These four have been consistently trying to find out further information for the past few months,' said the Director. 'We found them as a result of a..., let's just say it was a tip-off from Tony some two months ago. We have no idea who they are or why they're fishing but it seems too much of a coincidence that we have four at once, over a prolonged period, and I believe there must be a connection. Tony and Jim, I want you to investigate, but that's not the only reason we've invited you here this morning.'

A smirk played on most faces as they knew the word invite was the Director being polite. Part of the agreement when Tony, Jim, Ryan, Janine, Basil, and latterly, Fiona, had accepted their careers at the school was that their duties came first and if the Director said jump, the only question would be *how high?* For the Director and Violet there was no question that the school came first. It wasn't quite the same for Marion, but the Director and Violet knew that a happy wife meant a happy life and she was almost as crucial to the operation as the others. Although it wasn't vital for Marion to be at the meeting, she would eventually discover some of the information about the mission, so it made sense for her to be in attendance too.

They waited patiently for the Director to continue.

'I've already made the Home Secretary aware of this possible breach of security...'

'...But,' Jim interrupted.'

'Let me finish, Jim, then you can have your say. I'm almost certain this is more than coincidence and my gut tells me that these are going to be trouble. That's why the short-term mission is to find and stop these people before they can do any damage. And the long term... Janine, show the video.'

A clip from an entertainment news programme played on the screen. Ladies dressed in evening gowns and men in tuxedos walked the red carpet and stopped to pose for the paparazzi before entering the Guild Hall in London the night before. At a nod from the Director, Janine paused the video on a shot of Sir Paul Field, the majority shareholder of Arbuthnot and Lee – the cover firm that employees of the school worked for - and his wife, Lady Field, but known affectionately to the public as Lady Stacey. They all gave a brief smile at the vision of Lady Stacey who had once been a school employee but had now moved on.

It took great effort from Jim not to interrupt again. He knew the Director liked his games and, as he glanced at him, the boss looked around at the company to see their reactions. Violet, the only one who knew the whole plan looked down, trying to hide her smile. The others didn't have a clue what was going on and it was too far a stretch for them to put the pieces together. Yet.

At a look from the Director, Janine pressed the pause button and the video continued. The narrator voiced the proceedings.

'Sir Paul Field is expected to be announced as winner of the award. Arbuthnot and Lee has performed consistently well throughout the year and his employees rate the organisation as the number one place to work. Over to you, Marty...'

'Sir Paul,' Marty called, and the entrepreneur stopped and smiled. 'Why do you think your company's doing so well?'

'Because our employees are our best asset and we know how to treat them. We work hard for them and they return the compliment. Thank you.'

He turned to the cameras and posed for photographers along with his wife.

'Plans for anything new for the future, Sir Paul?'

'Watch this space, and the one at the end of Oxford Street.'

Many of the media had heard Sir Paul's response and crowded around him like flies around jam. Two large men in suits with small microphones in their ears appeared and made a space around the couple, stopping further intrusion by the journalists. Sir Paul ignored any further questions and they walked into the building, smiling and waving at the crowds outside before disappearing inside.

'You heard it here first,' said Marty. 'And now back to Roger in the studio...'

Janine stopped the video and all faces were on the Director.

'So, in a nutshell, our new facility is going to be in Oxford Street.'

The twins burst out laughing and the others looked at them in surprise.

'It's a twin thing,' said Fiona, *and probably something to do with Claire too*, she thought, but kept that to herself.

Even though they had no idea who three of the four snoopers were, it seemed too coincidental to Tony that his encounter with Tina could have been chance when he now knew that people were trying to find out more about the school.

*****

Violet was the only one who knew how unsettling the discovery was for the Director. 'I have a bad feeling about this,' he said to her when they were home having dinner that evening.

'You always say that, my love, whenever anyone tries to get information about the school.'

'Yes, but I was going to add that I have a bad feeling about this because they must have known enough about Tony to realise he was vulnerable so have already carried out a lot of research to get to this stage. That tells me there's money behind this, a lot of it. The man with the beard…' He stopped to think and Violet jumped in.

'The one wearing sunglasses and a hat with the woman named Tina? Is something ringing a bell?'

'He reminds me of someone, but I can't quite put my finger on it.'

'I'm not surprised. Most of his face and head was covered so he obviously didn't want anyone to recognise him.'

'Exactly, Violet. So he must be known to us. But the woman isn't, except to Tony that is, and she's not made any effort to hide or to disguise herself.'

129

They were both quiet for a few seconds, thinking about the consequences of the organisation's cover being blown. 'It's pretty obvious that they're determined to expose us for what we really are, and that could jeopardise our reputation, the move, future operations, and put the lives of many in danger,' Violet added.

'Probably ruin a number of politicians' reputations and put the lives of some of my contacts at risk too.' The Director sighed, as they contemplated the worst. 'What do you think, Vi?'

'We need to stop them, whatever it takes. And on a stricter than usual need to know basis. In fact, you're the only one who should know the full story, just in case.'

'I agree,' he said, getting up and kissing his wife on the cheek. 'I'll be in my study for the rest of the evening. Try not to worry.'

'I'll watch some crap TV,' she said. 'That should do the trick.'

The Director's first call was to an old school pal now living in Panama whose sister worked for Sir Paul, thanks to the Director.

'Good grief, is that you, Wizzer? Long-time no speak, old boy, how are you?'

'All's well here, Dingo,' the Director replied, happy to be using school nicknames as they usually did. Dingo was part of a small circle of less than ten people who still called him Wizz or Wizzer, more on account of his quick thinking and ability to resolve problems than his speed on the athletics track. 'I need to speak to you about a matter of some importance. Is this a good...'

'Don't worry, Wizzer. All calls on this line are secure. Is it about Fleabee? I only spoke to her last week and she was fine.'

'It's nothing to do with your sister, Dingo. I need some help.'

'Anything for you, my friend.'

'You might not say that when you know what it is.'

'Sounds intriguing. Is it legit?'

'Not exactly. I need some weapons, and drugs if you can get them, to be freighted from the terminal at Taboguilla Island to Antwerp.'

'Hmm. So you're calling in that favour from all those years ago?'

'If you want to call it that, yes. Think you can do it without getting caught?' the Director asked, knowing his old pal loved a challenge.

'I don't hear from you in eighteen months and you want to insult me too?' Dingo said, laughing. 'Might take a hefty amount of cash but I can do it. When do you need it?'

'ASAP.'

'Yeah, it would be. Stupid question, of course. Is Antwerp the final destination?'

'No, that'll be Felixstowe.'

'Do you want me to deal directly with Gareth in Antwerp? I take it the less contact you have to make the better?'

His old pal was quick on the uptake, as usual. 'Spot on, Dingo. I need them en route as soon as you can but don't have a delivery date to Felixstowe yet, I'll let you know when I get it.'

'Fair enough. I'll get right onto it and let you know how much I need as soon as I can.'

'I've already transferred £65k to your account, Dingo. Let me know when you need more.'

'Wiz by name and nature still!' Dingo laughed. 'That should be plenty for now.'

'Hmm, you've done this sort of thing before then?' The Director tried to hide his surprise.

'Let's just say I know the value of items on the black market. Just in case I need to. Leave it with me and I'll get back to you soon. I should be able to get the ball rolling this afternoon and update you tomorrow. Now how's the lovely Violet and aside from smuggling, what have you been getting up to lately.'

They spent a further ten minutes catching up on family and day to day matters before finishing the call. The Director felt more in control later when he joined Violet later to watch some inane programme about celebrity plastic surgery.

True to his word, Dingo called the following day. 'Seems that a number of weapons dealers live in this region and, funnily enough, they can get their hands on drugs too. I thought twenty rifles and a kilo of heroin might do the trick, so I went ahead and placed the order.'

Makes it sound like he's shopping in Tesco, the Director thought, before bringing his distracted mind back to the present.

'All up price, including shipping, is £85k. And the good news, is the ship will be in Brussels between twenty-eight and thirty-one days, as long as the shipping lanes stay as they are today. I'll let you know its ETA nearer the time.'

'Great stuff, Dingo, thanks. I'll transfer the rest of the cash later. I'll know the Felixstowe delivery date by the time you tell me the ETA, so we can arrange the final crossing then. And let me know if I can ever...'

'I think we're quits for now, Wiz. But, yeah, I'll bear it in mind. Give my best to Violet and the chums.'

'Will do.'

The next call was to Sir Paul Field. 'Hello, my friend,' said the Director. 'How do you feel about making another donation to our esteemed school and centre of operations? All tax deductible of course.'

Sir Paul chuckled. 'How much do you need?'

'I think £40k should do the trick this time.'

'Consider it done,' he said, happy to invest in both of their futures.

Chapter 8 – The Trap

'Let's start with the woman you slept with, then move onto the others,' said Jim.

Tony agreed to the plan-but it didn't quite work out that way.

They'd been given the names of three of the four people who'd been snooping around and, assuming these were false, they double-checked by using the company's facial recognition system. They didn't yet have any name for the bearded man and the facial recognition system didn't help on this occasion.

'Disguised? Maybe a false nose or something?' Tony suggested.

'Could be,' Jim said, rubbing his chin thoughtfully. 'We both know how to fool the most advanced system on the market, perhaps he does, too.'

As was usual with any investigations they carried out, once they had the names, the public internet was the first port of call to ascertain what information was available to any curious searchers. This was information that suspects wanted anyone to be able find.

Tony was surprised to find that Tina, the woman he'd met, had given him her proper name, or a shortened version of it anyway. He typed *Christina Jansen* into the search engine and got to work. Jim did the same. After searching for an hour, Tony leaned back in his chair. 'Absolutely nothing on the Christina Jansen, we're looking for,' he said. 'How about you?'

'Zilch,' Jim agreed. 'But I needed a break from looking for her so decided to look for some of the others. There's loads of info about Antonio and Vinnie Russo. They're identical twins, too, only these two appear to be well known in the criminal underworld. Look at all this, just from a quick Google search…'

Tony leaned over his brother's shoulder and looked at the screen. There were a number of websites detailing information about the criminals whose names were associated with gangs both in London and Naples.

'It's like they're taunting the authorities, or advertising their services,' Tony said. 'They're either completely stupid or arrogant. Or it could just be that they're criminal masterminds and it's unlikely they'll get caught.'

'Doubt that,' said Jim, pointing to something on the screen, and both laughed. A pop-up had appeared on the article they were reading citing the time the Russo twins had served at Her Majesty's pleasure for the crimes they'd committed.

'Not the sharpest tools in the box then,' Tony said, taking a USB stick out of his pocket. 'But after my complacency with Tina, I promise I'll take this seriously, even though making these two disappear should be a doddle.'

'Do you think it's likely that Christina's in charge then?' asked Jim.

As he thought about his brother's comment, Tony put the USB stick in his computer and typed in some instructions. The screen ran through an encryption sequence then Tony logged on to his email server. This wasn't the email that friends and family had but was part of the dark web; encrypted, hidden from searchers, and completely anonymous. He was pretty sure that nobody would be able to track down his location through the email, no matter how skilled or how hard they tried - he could be whoever he wanted. All those who were required to carry out investigative roles at the school had access to the dark web.

'If these Italians have links to the mafia, do you think they'd be happy to take orders from a woman?' he asked, as he typed.

'Orders? Probably not,' said Jim. 'But it looks like they'd be happy to take money from anyone. And if she has the money...?'

'Well, it looks like she's probably working with the guy with the beard, and one of those two is in charge.'

'I agree. So let's talk about our next move.'

'Surveillance first, as per the book, then, dependent on what we discover, phase two will be the sting.'

'I agree,' said Jim. 'Let's get cracking.'

The Russo twins thought they were good at disguising their electronic footprint, but Tony used his wizardry to track them down to the Greenwich area of South London. Their first visit was on a warm, late-spring Saturday when the area was buzzing with locals and tourists alike. Jim and Tony were surprised to discover that, from the address they'd been given by the school, the Russo twins were renting an apartment in an upmarket serviced complex. Disguised with wigs, moustaches and glasses, posing as tourists, they walked along the path, passing the famous observatory and the Maritime Museum, to the building where they'd seen the Russo twins enter and exit. There were numerous cafes and restaurants nearby and they chose a table where they could watch the building without being noticed.

It was a modern apartment block with a glass frontage, and each unit had a small balcony. The front facing balconies all had a view over the River Thames and the corner apartments had panoramic views across London.

'These won't be cheap to rent' said Tony, ticking things off on his fingers as he spoke. 'Lots of local facilities and attractions. Plenty of green space. Stunning views. Dead easy commute into the city. Last but not least, serviced, and with a manned reception to give added security.' He winked at his brother.

'We'll see,' Jim replied. 'But I certainly didn't expect to find them in such luxurious surroundings. And why would they base themselves almost six hundred miles from the place they're supposed to be investigating?'

'I didn't expect to find them here, either. But I daresay we'll soon find out.'

As they watched, Antonio Russo exited the door to the building.

'I've got him,' said Jim, downing the rest of his coffee and pushing back his chair.

'Hang on,' Tony said, motioning for his twin to sit. 'He's coming over here - yep, he's gone into the cafe next door.'

They surreptitiously watched as he appeared to place an order, then stepped outside and lit a cigarette. They were close enough to see a woman passing by give him a dirty look and him leaning in her direction, blowing smoke towards her face.

'Disgusting man!' the woman said, and Antonio chuckled.

'Charming,' said Tony, watching as Antonio threw his cigarette end to the floor, went back into the café to collect his food, then headed back towards the building. 'Do you want to check out that security just now?' he asked Jim.

'On it,' Jim replied, and Tony watched as his brother grabbed the door behind the target before it closed.

The man behind the reception desk briefly looked up from his phone when Jim entered the building behind the twin. He acknowledged them both with a nod, then returned his full attention to the phone. There were a few monitors on the right side of his desk, which Jim rightly assumed were the CCTV

137

camera feeds. Both men headed to the lifts and the target pressed the button. When the lift arrived, Jim went to follow the twin into the lift but the man shook his head.

'No. Get the next one,' he said.

Jim had expected to hear heavily accented English, but he sounded as cockney as Danny Dyer, and he masked the surprise that he felt.

Deciding not to draw attention to himself, Jim shrugged his shoulders and stepped back, but not before he'd seen the target press the button for floor five. As soon as the doors closed, he called another lift which arrived within a few seconds. As Jim left the lift on the fifth floor, he heard a door close at the end of the corridor. He hurried along it, noting the CCTV camera pointed in the direction of the lift and knowing the receptionist was too interested in his phone to do his job properly, Jim stood outside each of the end apartments in turn, trying to hear anything that was going on inside. The doors were thick and no sound came from them, so he headed back to the lifts less than a minute later. There were a few other people coming and going as he left the building, but the receptionist took no notice of any of them, mesmerised with whatever he was looking at on his phone.

'How did it go?' Tony asked, as Jim came back to sit at the table in the café. They ordered a second coffee and pretended to scan their tourist leaflets. 'Do we need to go in as workmen?'

'Nah. The bloke on the desk took hardly any notice. They have CCTV but he wasn't looking at that either. Don't know if they're all like that but we can either do a few more recces or take a chance. I narrowed their apartment down to two, so it's 50/50 when we go in.'

After covertly watching the building for a further fifteen minutes, Tony and Jim were about to

138

call it a day when they struck lucky: the Russo twins left the building, heading in the direction of the riverboat. Tony and Jim watched as they joined the queue, then Jim made a quick call to Ryan.

'They're going to get the riverboat. Can you take it from here?'

Ryan said he could, and Jim raised an eyebrow at Tony. There was no time like the present and his brother's slight nod confirmed that he agreed, without either having to say a word.

'We're going in, Ryan. If it looks like they've changed their minds or have forgotten something, let us know.'

'Will do,' Ryan confirmed, and ended the call.

A very helpful woman who was leaving the building held the door open for them.

'Thank you,' said Tony, smiling politely. They followed two men into the lift who selected the third floor. Jim pressed the button for floor seven and they all proceeded to ignore each other until the doors opened and the other men left. Getting out on the seventh floor, the twins found the stairwell marked *Emergency Exit* at the corner of the building and headed to the fifth floor. About to open the door to go into the main corridor, the sound of voices stopped them. The occupants of one of the corner apartments were leaving. The twins peered through a window in the door watching the couple who were leaving, and noting their linked hands. The woman smiled up at the man and kissed him, then they headed towards the lifts.

'Do you think they saw us,' Jim asked, a twinkle in his eye. Tony didn't bother to reply. *They wouldn't notice if a giraffe walked past them,* he thought.

When they were satisfied there was nobody else about, they left the stairwell and headed for the door opposite the young couple's apartment. Tony shaded his brother and watched the corridor as Jim got to work on the lock. It wasn't particularly sophisticated and there was a satisfying click within two minutes.

It had been a while since Jim had used this particular skill and his brother was pleasantly surprised. 'Haven't lost your touch then?' he said, as they entered the apartment. They quickly donned latex gloves and worked fast.

A laptop had been left open and it sat on a table next to a settee in the living area. Tony pressed the arrow down button, and it came to life – they hadn't even switched it off. He took a dongle out of his pocket and started transferring information to it. As well as searching the apartment, Jim hid a few bugs so they could monitor all conversations and activity taking place there. Minutes later, they left the apartment, walked back up to the seventh floor and took the lift down to the foyer.

They returned to their own digs in a less luxurious part of South London and Tony loaded the information gained from the Russo twins onto his own laptop. While he spent time reading and making notes, Jim made a few calls to Ryan and the office, using his encrypted phone.

'They already have a local and like to drink at the Black Horse,' said Ryan.

'Do all the punters know each other?' Jim asked.

'No, mate. It's your typical London boozer, which should make it easier for Janine. And I'll be on hand just in case she needs me. We're going to do it tomorrow night.'

'Great, Ryan. Good luck, although I know you won't need it.'

His next call was to the school. Violet answered and he quickly explained what they'd done so far, and what was going to happen the following night.

'Tony will email the report to the Director on Monday afternoon with an outline of a plan we should have by then.'

*****

Ryan entered the Black Horse and sat at the bar. Like Tony and Jim, he was disguised; he now had a beard, a prosthetic nose, glasses and a body suit that fattened up his muscular body.

'Pint of lager, please,' he said to the barman, taking out his iPad. *I'll be seeing double in my sleep at this rate,* thought Ryan, watching the identical twins who were sitting at a table adjacent to the other side of the bar. He messaged the information to Janine who entered the bar, strutting her stuff. All heads turned at the leggy blonde. She sat at the other end of the bar and the two barmen jostled to see who could get to her first.

'Spritzer please,' she said to the winner, giving him a smile. 'Dry white.'

'Can I get you anything else, darling?' he asked when he put her drink down on the bar.

'No thanks,' she said, noticing one of the twins approaching the bar with his and his brother's empty glasses.

'Actually, you may be able to give me some advice,' Janine said as Vinnie Russo put his empty glasses on the bar and looked at the barman, who ignored him. 'I'm looking for somewhere local to rent. You know, a nice place.'

'Maybe I can help with that,' Vinnie interrupted. 'Two pints please, mate,' he said to the barman, to get him out of the way before turning back to Janine. 'Me and my brother rent an apartment in River Tower. Luxury fixtures and fittings, stunning views, and a great location.'

141

'Oh, you sound like an estate agent,' she said, and they both laughed. 'Do you have any photos I can see?' she asked.

Vinnie put his android phone on the bar. 'The Black Horse WIFI's a bit slow,' he said, 'but just bear with me.'

Result! thought Janine as she watched him tap on his phone for a minute or so.

'I haven't taken any photos, but the website is…'

'I can't quite make it out,' she said leaning into his back. 'Can I see?'

Ryan watched from the other end of the bar, trying to subdue his emotions while his wife came on to the target.

Janine held out her hand and Vinnie passed her his phone. Pretending to study the website, Janine got to work straight away. As she ooh'd and aah'd and said, 'Wow, they look great!,' she installed a phone spy app while he was looking at her, and not the phone. Now the information on his mobile could be accessed remotely by Janine's own device. The heads on the twins' beers were going visibly flat and Ryan saw the second twin becoming impatient. He also knew Janine needed a few more minutes.

Antonio got up from his seat and headed towards the bar. Ryan got up off his stool and started staggering, bumping into Antonio as he did so.

'I'm sorry, mate,' he said, swaying slightly. 'Didn't see you there.'

'Didn't see me? You must be blind then, as well as pissed!'

'Pished! Pished! I'm not fucking pished, mate. I said sorry okay. You want to make something of it?'

'Think you'd have a fucking chance do you, big fella?' Antonio looked up into Ryan's eyes, his temper now getting the better of him. 'You don't know who

142

you're fucking dealing with, arsehole.' He pushed Ryan and when Vinnie and the barman saw Ryan ball his hand into a fist and lean back about to punch Antonio, they ran the short distance to them both.

Her work finished, Janine put Vinnie's phone on the bar, grabbed her bag and left via the pub's rear entrance that she'd recce'd the day before.

'No need for that. Come on, you,' the barman said to Ryan. 'Sling your hook. And you, calm the fuck down.'

Ryan staggered to the door and left the pub while the twins went to the bar and picked up their pints.

'Where's she gone?' asked Vinnie.

'Probably didn't want any trouble, mate,' the barman said. 'At least she didn't nick your phone.'

'Damn,' Vinnie said, 'looked like she was up for it too.' He picked up his phone and checked all was well, just in case. *They'd have to get up early to pull one over on Vinnie Russo,* he thought, smiling to himself. He put the phone back in his pocket.

*****

'We need to lure them into our web, make them an illegal offer they can't refuse, and then set the trap,' Tony said. 'I have an idea, but we're going to need a little help to set it up and it may take a week or two.'

'Oh do tell,' said Jim, doing his best impression of a luvvie, and Tony outlined his plan.

With a little help from some of techy guys at the company, ten days later the drug dealer Giovanni Vitali looked as if he were an established presence on the dark web. If someone searched for him on the internet, they would discover that Giovanni was an alleged mafia member from Southern Italy, had been educated in England where his parents lived periodically, had served a short prison sentence for

143

fraud, and was suspected of involvement in other crimes; there was a note about information on the latter being redacted due to data protection laws. They would struggle to find any further information, but those with access to the dark web could find out more, such as weapons, drugs and hit men they could hire from Giovanni – at a premium price - and what they could expect if they double-crossed him. Cheekily, there were also a list of job vacancies in his company, for positions that his family members couldn't fill. Jim and Tony presented the results of the team's hard work to the Director who, through his own list of contacts, set about finding flaws in Giovanni's online identity.

Two days later the last response was sent to the Director. None of the seven he had contacted were able to find any errors or weaknesses in the information, and if they hadn't already known he was fake, would have believed otherwise.

'So, Operation End-Game is a go,' the Director said, giving the twins the green light and a code name for their work. 'Do your stuff and let's see how long it takes these two to fall into the trap. But be careful. You know how easy it can be to create a false internet presence. These twins may not be as stupid as they seem.'

'Will do,' the brothers answered in unison and returned to their own offices in the school.

'*End Game*, eh?' said Tony as he typed the email and made a few amendments after showing his brother. 'Guess it's because it's the last full Op from this location. Not very imaginative though.'

'Just get on with it,' said Jim, ignoring his brother's chatter.

A few minutes later, after a final double-check, Tony finished typing and hit send.

They received a response from Antonio Russo less than twenty-four hours later.

'Enough time for them to check out our man's validity,' said Jim, 'but also not too long to annoy him for not responding sooner. What does it say?'

Tony opened the email: *Dear Giovanni. Thank you for considering me and my brother for this job. We're happy to meet with you to discuss terms. Please let me know a number to call so the arrangements can be made.*

You won't be disappointed.

It was signed *The brothers Russo* with a logo of a black raven underneath.

'Hook, line and sinker,' said Jim. 'The game begins.'

They purchased a number of burner phones to use and emailed the number of one for the Russo twins to contact them. The meeting was set-up to take place the following day, outside London, on the land next to a factory that had gone bankrupt during the recession five years before.

'This is it,' said Ryan as he parked the limousine behind the factory, ensuring it couldn't be seen from the road or by people travelling by train. 'And look, they're here already.' His passengers, in the back of the vehicle, looked towards where their targets were standing, chatting and smoking. 'Shall we?' said Ryan.

Tony stayed in the back of the car and as Jim got out, he said, 'Yes, Mr Vitali, will do.'

The Russo twins heard. Both men dropped the cigarettes they were smoking, scuffed them out with their feet and looked towards the car at the two men who were walking towards them.

'Dino,' said Jim, offering his hand for the twins to shake. 'I'm Mr Vitali's nephew. And this is Luca.'

'Antonio and Vinnie,' Antonio replied as they all shook hands. 'Isn't Giovanni coming?'

Dino and Luca looked at each other in disbelief. Luca's face hardened into a scowl. 'Show some respect, Vinnie. Mr Vitali doesn't like over-familiarity. If you want to work for him, you play by Mr Vitali's rules. Do we understand each other?'

Vinnie, the calmer of the two, felt his brother starting to twitch. He jumped in before Antonio had a chance to ruin this relationship before it started.

'We understand, Luca. What does Mr Vitali have in mind for us and how did he find out about our work?'

'Are you trying to wind me up, eh? You think Mr Vitali is stupid? That he doesn't have the capability to find out about people who he might want to bring into the fold? Jeez!' Luca bashed his forehead with his palm.

'Come on, Luca, this was a mistake. Let's go,' Dino said. Both men turned and began to walk back towards the car.

'Hey, Dino, Luca. Hang on.'

A smile played on Jim's lips, but he hid it as they stopped and turned back to face the twins.

'No offence meant,' Antonio said. 'But you can't be too careful these days. Can you tell us what we can do for Mr Vitali and maybe what he can do for us?'

'We have a shipment coming in shortly that needs collecting and distributing. Mr Vitali said if you do a good job with this one, there'll be more work in the future. Think about it and phone me in the hour if you want the job.'

'Will do,' said Vinnie. 'And give Mr Vitali our regards.'

Jim and Ryan walked away knowing the trap was set. As expected, the phone rang and the Russo's accepted before the hour was up.

'I can't believe how easy it was,' Jim told Tony as they left the area and headed in the direction of their apartment. 'They couldn't be more stupid if they had a degree in stupidity. Ryan was like an extra in a mafia movie. His performance was worthy of an Oscar!'

'Bravo, Ryan.'

The men laughed.

'It's not done yet, but it did seem too easy. Let's hope the sting goes as planned next week.' Ryan said.

Some ten minutes later they said their goodbyes and the twins left the car and headed for the station. They used public toilets to remove their facial disguises before getting the tube the three stops to their station.

Back at the apartment, Jim quickly wrote up the report and sent it to the Director.

Tony, Jim, Ryan and Janine took it in turns to monitor the Russo twins' movements during the next few days, alternating between following them and checking Vinnie Russo's phone activity and the computer used by both twins.

'Haven't had so much fun in ages,' Tony said to Janine. They were on duty in the apartment. He yawned and stretched, then stood up and paced up and down the room.

'For Pete's sake, you're doing my head in. You're like a caged lion or something. Why don't you go out for some fresh air? I'll let you know if anything interesting comes through.'

'Good idea.' Tony put on his coat and was about to leave the apartment when there was a ping from the computer.

'Hang on,' Janine said as she opened the email addressed to Vinnie. It was a one liner and said simply: *Phone me.* They didn't bother trying to trace the email while they waited for Vinnie to use his phone.

Tony's phone rang. 'They've just returned to their apartment,' Jim said.

'Vinnie's about to call someone,' Janine replied to her husband. 'We'll listen in to the conversation and will let you know the outcome.'

As soon as the call finished, Janine put up her hand and they heard the ringing tone. The phone was answered on the third ring by a man with a slight French accent.

'Hello, An…'

'Don't use my name and just listen to me. My source tells me they're scaling down their operations during the next few months. There's talk of a move too. Do the next recce of the facility on Wednesday; he also told me they're due a big staff meeting then and it's unusual for them to have it there. I want photos of all those going in and out. Photos of the private vehicles and any removal trucks too. Make sure you get their licence plates. I need to be able to track everything to a company or an owner. Got it?'

'Got it,' said Vinnie. 'You want a thorough job without us getting caught. No probs. We'll go up on Tuesday. And the money?'

'I'll pay you when I see the photographs, and not before. And I'll contact you,' the voice said before terminating the call.

'Time for the Russo's to make a decision,' said Tony, 'and Mr Vitali has to make it worth their while.'

*****

As he'd promised, Dingo contacted the Director about the shipment. 'It's due to arrive on Saturday. The LFC Juynis docks into Felixstowe every third Wednesday for the next four months. It takes four days and Gareth tells me he can do a quick turnaround from Antwerp if you like? He can get the container on Sunday, so it'll arrive next Wednesday. Or I can ask him to arrange to store it for you until you're ready? Just let me know.

'Thanks, Dingo and will do. Let me make a few calls and I'll get back to you.'

As soon as they'd finished the call, the Director's phone rang. 'One of their contacts wants the

Russo twins to recce the school next Wednesday,' Tony said, getting straight to the point. 'We're working on the number and should have a name to you by close of play today. But they've been told to travel up on Tuesday, take as many photos of all the comings and goings on Wednesday, and they also know about our meetings.'

So we have a mole to deal with. 'I see,' said the Director. 'We'll deal with the mole later, but this timing is perfect. Tell them you need them to do a job at Felixstowe port on Wednesday, Tony, timings to follow. See if they'll take the bait straight away. If not, offer them what you have to, to make them do it. But start with small money and no more than 10k – you can transfer five now and the rest on completion of the job if you have to go that high. Get Jim to make promises about a place in Mr Vitali's network in the future, blah blah. You know the score.'

'Will do. And what about the timings?'

'It'll be Wednesday night, but I'll get all the details and let you know. I don't want the targets to know until a few hours before.'

'Got it, boss. We'll get right onto it.'

While the Russo's were getting ready to go out on Thursday night, Tony and Janine were monitoring their conversations from Tony and Jim's apartment.

'Maybe that tasty bird will be there again,' Vinnie said. 'Fancy my chances there.'

'Too classy for you, little bruv,' Antonio responded, and the listeners heard some static.

'He must have cuffed him or something. That's what I would have done.'

Janine nodded and they carried on listening.

'Can't believe we've got tickets for a home match on Saturday! What's the plan?' Antonio asked and they spent a few minutes discussing Arsenal's forthcoming match against their rivals, Tottenham Hotspur.

'Kick off's at 3 o'clock,' Vinnie replied, 'so let's make a day of it. We'll leave here…'

The rest of the conversation was cut off as Tony and Janine heard the door of the apartment close. Ryan and Jim were outside, and Janine called Ryan.

'They've just left the apartment and are heading for the Black Horse. Don't see any point in following them tonight.'

'I agree,' said Ryan. 'We'll see you at the apartment.'

When they met at Tony and Jim's apartment later, Janine repeated the conversation they'd heard, and Tony and Jim started to laugh.

'Come on then, we're not all psychic. You're going to have to tell us what you're thinking.'

Ryan cottoned on and started laughing too.

'Is someone going to tell me what's going on?'

'It's a bloke thing, my love. But we're going to arrange to meet them on Saturday afternoon. When they should be at the match. We'll see how keen they are to work for Mr Vitali.'

Jim made the call and Vinnie answered.

'Vinnie, it's Dino. Can you talk?'

'We're in the pub. Can you give me two minutes?'

Jim waited until the background noise dissipated. 'I'm outside now and nobody's about.'

'I have more details of the job Mr Vitali wants you to do but I can't discuss it on the phone. Mr Vitali wants to meet you on Saturday to tell you about it. Same place at two o'clock.'

'Two o'clock on Saturday? Can we make it…'

'Yeah, that's right, two o'clock. Is that a problem for you, Vinnie? You do want to work for Mr Vitali, don't you?'

150

'Ah, yes, it's just that…Nothing, we'll be there at two o'clock on Saturday.'

Vinnie smoked a cigarette before going back into the pub, delaying having to listen to his brother's reaction when he gave him the news.

*****

Obtaining details of the man Vinnie Russo had called took longer than they'd promised the Director. The phone had already been disposed of and it took the investigators time to track the number back to the purchaser. Janine was well aware that the man who bought it might not be the man involved with the Russo's, so wanted to check him out prior to passing details to the Director. Using an untraceable URL, she Googled his name.

'Wow!' she said to herself when the search returned a tonne of information, not only about Andre Robertson, but also about his father, a rich and powerful entrepreneur. She called the Director on a secure, encrypted phone line.

'Andre Robertson,' she said once they'd dispensed with the niceties. 'The son of *the* Andrew Robertson. Looks like he's heading up their investigation, and I assume it's at the request of his father.'

'Good work, Janine, thanks. We'll deal with Mr Robertson and Miss Jansen as soon as the Russo twins are out of the way. Inform the others and I'll be in touch.'

*****

The Russo's were there as promised on Saturday, but this time Tony watched and listened from a distance as Jim and Ryan met them.

The men shook hands again.

'Is Mr Vitali coming?' Antonio asked.

'He said sorry, but he had a last-minute invitation to watch the Arsenal match.'

151

'The Arsenal match?' Antonio asked, his face reddening. The warning look Vinnie gave his brother wasn't lost on the other men, but they chose to ignore it.

'An invitation from a business associate he accepted at the last minute. Do you guys like football? Mr Vitali said if you do a good job for him, he'll get you season tickets for your club.'

'Season tickets for Arsenal?' said Vinnie.

'We were going to the match today,' his brother added, his face softening on hearing the words 'season tickets'. 'Mr Vitali can get us season tickets for the Arsenal? For real?'

'Yeah, for real. So let's talk business and maybe you can make it to the second half. We have a number of shipments arriving at Felixstowe this coming Wednesday. We'll both be there to…'

'Wednesday?'

'If you don't let me fucking finish, Vinnie, you won't get to see any of the Arsenal match today.'

Vinnie opened his mouth to speak but thought better of it. He balled his hands into fists and then unballed them, determined to contain his temper.

Dino continued. 'We have two ships arriving. Me and Luca have three different shipments to deal with so we want you to take charge of one shipment coming in from Antwerp. We don't know the ETA yet but will give you a call on Tuesday with all the information you need. *Now* you can ask any questions.'

'So we bring the van, sign for the shipment, and deliver the goods to Mr Vitali's customers? Is that about right?'

'That's it exactly.' Luca replied this time. 'The shipment will have already gone through customs and we'll give you the names and addresses of the customers when we meet up on Tuesday night. You can either drive down to Felixstowe on Wednesday morning or stay overnight on Tuesday.'

'It has to be this Wednesday?' Vinnie asked.

'Shall I phone the fucking shipping line, Vinnie, and ask them to delay the arrival date?' Dino said, with a smile, and they all laughed. 'Do you boys want the job or not?'

'Can we talk about payment?'

'My uncle has authorised payments of four grand now and four when the job's completed and don't forget the season tickets. If you do a good job for him, he wants to meet up and talk about more permanent roles in the future. He needs two people to run one of his clubs and your names were mentioned.'

The men exchanged a look and Jim knew they were doing the same as he did with Tony. It was a twin thing and they'd come to a decision without having to speak to each other.

'Thank Mr Vitali for his generosity,' Antonio said. 'We're in.'

'Good. Let me know when you want to go to Felixstowe.'

'We'll go on Tuesday, Dino, and stay over.'

'Good,' said Dino. 'I'll give you a call on Tuesday morning with the hotel details and the ship's ETA, and let you know where and when to pick up the hire van. Enjoy the rest of the match.'

The twins said their goodbyes and Jim and Ryan watched as they hotfooted it towards the railway station.

Now the trap was set, they were able to reduce the surveillance on the twins, but the Director wanted to know how the Russo's planned to handle the clash of jobs. On Sunday, Janine and Ryan took the day off and Jim and Fiona were spending the day together, so Tony monitored the conversations from the Russo's. They didn't surface until after eleven am.

'Coffee. My head's banging.'

Tony recognised the voice as Antonio's.

There was movement but not much conversation so he assumed the men were drinking their coffee in silence. When they were starting to come around, they discussed Arsenal's win before dealing with their dilemma. That came after they'd had their second coffee.

'He's going to be fucking furious.'

'I know. But this is too good to pass up,' Vinnie replied to his brother. 'And if we're already working for Mr Vitali, by the time he realises we haven't done the job, he won't want to mess with us.'

'My thoughts exactly. So we don't tell him?'

'We don't tell him, Antonio, and we ignore his calls. We'll get new phones and change our numbers so he can't contact us. If he bothers to find out where we are, we'll have the support of Mr Vitali and his heavies and Andre's a lightweight compared to them. He wouldn't be stupid enough to come after us.'

'You're right, but he might send the crazy woman.'

'Like I said, by then we'll be on Mr Vitali's management team.'

The twins had a lazy Sunday and spent Monday going over various scenarios of the job on Wednesday.

*****

It was six pm and the LFC Juynis had already docked at Felixstowe. The area around the ship was lit up like a Christmas tree and men and machines were going about their business, looking like an army of worker ants from a distance. The Director had made a number of calls and plain clothed members of the National Crime Agency were hiding within the port around the ship's offloading bays, their main effort was concentrated on storage area 135, where a team of armed police were also in waiting.

Vinnie's phone rang and he gave his brother the paperwork while he took it out of his pocket to answer. 'It's Dino,' said Jim. 'The ship's Cargo Master will meet you outside building 135. Show him the paperwork Luca gave you. The inventory lists vehicle parts, but these numbers correspond to the number of weapons in the boxes. Ask him to leave you to it while you do your check, then when you're satisfied the numbers match those on the paperwork, call him back and sign for them. If the numbers don't match that means someone has double-crossed Mr Vitali. Call me and let me know if this is the case, but still carry out the deliveries on the list, top to bottom.'

'Got it.'

Armed with their instructions, Vinnie and Antonio strutted around until they found building 135 and the Cargo Master arrived a few minutes later.

'Paperwork please.' He was all business and the twins gave him their documents. Satisfied, the man signed at the bottom, returned the documents to them and passed paperwork to them. 'Sign here,' he pointed, 'and here.'

'We'll check the contents first then give you a call.'

'As you wish,' the man said. The Russos followed him into the building where the cargo covered the floor, top to bottom. 'These three are yours.' He pointed to boxes and the twins checked the numbers again, ensuring that they matched the numbers on their paperwork. 'Call me when you're ready. I'll try not to keep you waiting, but I'm a busy man.' He strode off before they had a chance to reply. As soon as he was out of sight of the building, he made a call. 'They're in and like sitting ducks,' he said.

Antonio took the padlock keys out of his pocket and opened the first box. They counted the weapons as instructed. Like two boys playing at gangsters, they couldn't resist posturing with a few of the weapons and took photos of each other posing as hard men.

'I could get used to this,' Antonio said, laughing.

The novelty wore off towards the bottom of the second box when Vinnie felt something that wasn't the same as the other packing he'd removed.

'Hang on a minute. What's this?'

He pulled out the small bag and held it up so they could both look at it. The white substance looked like sugar or talcum powder. 'That, my brother, is either heroine or coke,' Antonio said, 'which Dino didn't mention.'

'Do you think it's a plant and they're trying to catch us out?' The twins looked at each other, both wondering whether they could get away with a bit of business of their own without Mr Vitali and his grunts finding out.

'Let's see how many there are,' Antonio said, and the laughter of a few minutes earlier was forgotten about as they were now all business.

Vinnie made the call when they'd finished. 'All cargo correct, Dino, but there's also something extra in the boxes. Small bags of coke or heroine.'

'Really? How many?'

Vinnie looked at his brother who nodded. 'Five.'

He waited for Dino to respond but was met with silence. 'Are you still there?'

'Yes. I'll come and get the bags. You contact the Cargo Master, sign for the other goods, load the crates and get cracking on the deliveries.'

'We're going up in the world, bro,' Vinnie said after the call was finished. 'Let's call this a bonus from

156

Mr Vitali.' He waved the small bag believing their new boss would be none the wiser, having not expected any drugs to be in with the weapons.

'Put it back in one of the crates and lock it.'

'No way. This little baby isn't leaving my side,' he said, putting the bag in the inside pocket of his jacket.

Ten minutes later, the door opened and three men entered, and walked towards them. They were surprised that it wasn't either Dino or the Cargo Master.

'Vincent and Antonio…'

'Shit,' said Vinnie, and both men looked around for an escape route. Any secondary escape routes were blocked by boxes and crates so the twins, perfectly in sync, made a joint subconscious decision. As they broke into a run, two of the three men in front of them raised their pistols and pointed them at the twins.

'Stop!' shouted the third man, but the twins had already done so, holding poses like cartoon characters stopped in mid-flow.

'Hands in the air, gentlemen. Search them, Gary,' the third man said, taking a radio out of his pocket. 'Zero this is one, get the uniforms in here.'

Gary did as he'd been ordered while the second man kept his weapon trained on the twins. 'Looks like heroine, boss, about a kilo and here's the keys.' As he spoke, the twins watched as four policemen entered the building, tooled up in bullet proof vests, weapons on their shoulders and various items on their belts.

'I'm arresting you both for possession of weapons and Class A drugs…' said the boss and the twins switched off to the words as they were cuffed and led toward the door while their rights were read to them.

Outside, they watched Dino walking towards the building and he could have been a professional actor as his face registered surprise at the scene in front of him. He turned around and started running away. Seeing him being apprehended before turning the corner gave the twins some small satisfaction. They had no idea what the prison sentence was for weapons and drugs trafficking but knew it would be some time before they saw the light of day again. Both knew they would do and say anything to make that time as short as they could.

*****

Andre was surprised he hadn't heard from the Russo twins by Thursday lunchtime and even more surprised when somebody else answered Vinnie's phone. Without thinking, he asked where Vinnie was.

Tony now knew exactly who he was speaking to and replied conversationally. 'Banged up in a police cell, awaiting trial.'

Andre's brain worked overtime, assuming they'd been caught trespassing while doing the job for him. It made him hesitate for a second and Tony decided to have some fun.

'Say hello to your girlfriend for me and tell her she didn't hide the bugs well enough. It was pretty much a waste of her time spending that night with me. Boy, we had a fun night though. She knows which buttons to press if you get my meaning…' The phone went dead. 'He's hung up on me Jim, I wonder why?'

Jim laughed and shook his head at his brother, neither one knowing that Andre had been looking forward to becoming a father, and not realising the chain of events that Tony's words would start.

Chapter 9 – Amsterdam

Christina was tired. The visits from Witch had lessened during her pregnancy and that had been the best thing about it-and the only part she would miss when her little girl arrived. Coming out of the bathroom, she knew there was something wrong as soon as she looked at Andre. His face was ashen.

'What on earth's the matter, Andre? You look ill. Has something happened?'

He was looking at her as if he didn't know her and Christina felt her pulse quicken and her hands started to feel clammy.

Andre crossed the space between them at lightning speed and slapped her hard across the face.

'Ow!' she screamed, falling back against the wall from the force of it.

She slid down to the floor, initially shocked by the onslaught; a shock quickly turned to anger. 'How dare you do that to me!' she screamed again. Still in disbelief, Christina put her hand against her stinging cheek 'How could you? What if I fell? You could have killed our baby! Why, Andre? Why?'

'Our baby? Are you sure about that Christina?'

He left the question hanging. Christina stood up slowly and walked unsteadily into the kitchen saying nothing as she recalled the morning she'd woken up in a stranger's bed. A few memories of the night had come back in bits and pieces later, as they often did after Witch had taken over. She started to feel her presence now and silently told her, 'I told you months ago I should have left him.'

'We can do better than that,' the demon replied.

'So you've got nothing to say? You've been unfaithful and lied to me all these months? I know it's not our baby!'

159

'You were unfaithful first!' Christina said.

'What?'

'In Amsterdam. I know you slept with another woman in Amsterdam.'

It took him completely by surprise and the guilt momentarily wiped the anger from his face. It was only for a second, but long enough for Christina to know she was right.

'That was completely different…' He looked at her in disbelief. 'I wanted to be able to please you like you did me…'

'You're not even denying it?'

'You can't compare me sleeping with a prostitute to you having another man's baby and lying to me about it, Christina. It's a totally different level of deceit.'

'Adultery is adultery, Andre, but remember, you told me to use any means to get those bugs into that house, so I was only doing what you told me to. But it doesn't matter now, we're finished.'

'I can't believe that you're turning this around on me! But like you say, it doesn't matter-too damn right we're finished. And you're not finishing it, I am!'

'That's where you're wrong, Andre. I'm putting an end to this as I should have when you came home from Amsterdam. Now get out.'

Andre's mouth opened and shut like a fish out of water, bewildered at her attitude.

'Go on,' she said. 'You've got ten minutes to pack your bags.'

'You're telling me to get out?' He felt his face redden and his disbelief turn to anger. 'You really think that I'm going to leave the apartment that I rented for us both? I've paid for absolutely everything! You are one seriously deranged woman.'

'Get out, Andre, or face the consequences,' said Witch, deciding it was time she took full control.

160

He felt a shiver from the sinister words and, seeing the look in her eyes change, knew it was time to put a stop to any further discussion. Trying his best to keep his hands off her, Andre spoke in a calm, measured tone. 'Pack your bags, Christina and get out of my apartment. I never want to see you again.'

He didn't see it coming. When Witch pulled the knife from behind her back and thrust it into his chest, he looked at her face, then at the knife, in horror.

She watched as the life drained from Andre's face and the blood from his body. He slumped to the floor and she didn't need to check his pulse to know he was dead.

'I need a lie down after that,' Witch said. She walked to the bedroom, laid on the bed and closed her eyes. She was asleep in less than a minute.

Andre's ringing phone woke Christina and she knew it hadn't been a bad dream as she walked to the kitchen and saw his body lying on the floor in a pool of blood. Christina recalled the research she'd carried out on her own mother's death and realised that her lover had met the same fate. She sank to the floor, put her head in her hands and wailed. *Why are some people blessed with lives full of joy and good fortune, yet mine moves from one catastrophe to another?* She continued to ignore the ringing phone, balled her hands into fists, and banged them on the floor until she was spent. When Christina stood up some time later her legs were unsteady as she walked to where his phone lay, next to his body. She checked the caller ID which showed his mother had called; she dropped the phone as she threw up on the floor next to Andre.

'Disgusting,' Witch said. 'You're so weak.'

Christina tried to ignore her as the panic at what had happened overtook any logical thought. Nobody would believe that it wasn't her and she'd spend the rest of her life in prison. Her daughter would

161

be taken away and she'd never see her grow or know who she was. And what if…

'Stop!' The demon screamed at her. 'Use his phone to text his mother. Tell her he'll phone at the weekend. Have a shower then pack everything you need. We're leaving.'

For once, Christina didn't argue.

Two days later, Christina passed her passport out of the car window to the customs official prior to driving onto the ferry at Calais. She'd paid the counterfeiter a fortune for the passport but was confident he'd done a good job and in his work, no questions were asked. The official checked the photo against the woman who presented the document. Although women changed their hair styles frequently, this one's short black bob style matched the one on her passport, as did her striking blue eyes. 'Enjoy your trip, Mrs Waterson,' he said.

'It's Miss,' she replied, and then said, 'I'll try.' She rubbed her belly, which looked like the baby would pop out of it at any second.

Arriving at Dover, she typed the name of the private hospital into the satnav and headed straight for London, hoping her labour wouldn't start before she arrived.

*****

While Christina was on her way to the UK, the twins were driving around Amsterdam, honing in on the location of the last mobile phone that Andre had used to phone the Russos. They had triangulated the phone's location a few days earlier, before it went dead, and having made some discreet enquiries, were now set up in the apartment block opposite, with a direct view into Andre's home. But nothing moved. After two days of surveillance with no sign of life, they decided to break in.

The downstairs foyer wasn't manned, but the door was secure. Having recce'd the area, they discovered there were CCTV cameras in the building. Always careful, for the recce they'd adopted the same disguises they'd used to follow the Russo brothers, but this time they decided to pose as workmen in case they had to break into the building. They planned to enter during a busy period when residents were leaving to start their day at work. It worked like a dream and a man absentmindedly held the door open as he was leaving. He was already gone before Tony said, 'Dank je wel'.

Andre's apartment was the penthouse on the 20th floor at the top of the building. After a quick check, they were satisfied that there were no CCTV cameras and the emergency exit door was a few steps from the lift lobby, should they need to use it. The smell of death hit them before they saw Andre's body, and a cursory glance confirmed their initial estimation that he had been dead for at least a few days.

'I wonder who did this? And where's the woman?' Jim asked, as he turned on the air conditioning in an attempt to get rid of the smell before they had a quick look around the apartment.

'It doesn't look like anything's missing.'

'A crime of passion, maybe?' He hoped not as that would mean the woman he'd slept with could be a murderer and, despite his dangerous job, the thought of sharing such intimacy with a murderer gave Tony the creeps. His brother shrugged and started a more thorough search of the apartment. Tony loaded Andre's computer and got to work. It took twenty minutes to gain access and he worked as fast as he could to discover any information Andre might have gathered about the school.

'The guy must have been a neat freak,' Tony said, as he found that all of the folders were named, dated, and well organised. Andre had called the top-level folder *Glenmalvern;* underneath there were sub folders entitled *background, photographs, personnel,* and *media releases.* Although not wanting to hang around indefinitely, Tony's curiosity got the better of him and while he was downloading the contents onto a USB stick, he checked out the folder entitled *personnel.*

'Holy crap!'

'Are you starring in a Batman movie or something?' Jim replied. 'What's up?'

'Our names are in this folder, along with all the other key staff, and there's personal information about the Director going back years, from the time he was in Uni. And a file about Sir Paul Field and his wife. I just hope this hasn't been sent anywhere.'

'How long will it take to check and delete all traces?'

'Longer than is safe to stay here,' Tony replied, removing the USB stick, shutting down the laptop and putting it into his rucksack. 'This is the safest way. We can't risk it getting into the wrong hands.'

'Hopefully the police or family will assume it was taken by whoever killed him,' Jim agreed and carried on with his search. 'I've found nothing relating to the school and he seems to be as organised with his physical stuff as his electronic.'

'Anything on the walls?'

'No hidden safe, so we're clear. The main bedroom is untidy. There's women's clothing strewn over the bed, and make up. It looks to me like someone left in a hurry.'

'It's pointing to the girlfriend, isn't it?'

'Looks that way, Tony. Come on, let's get out of here.' Jim turned off the aircon and they headed for the lift lobby. There was a *ping* as they waited, and the brothers ducked into the emergency exit area, not wanting to give away their position.

'Hurry up, man,'

They heard a man's voice with a Scottish Highlands lilt as clear as day, then the jangling of keys. Shortly after, a door closed and there was silence. They ran down four sets of stairs then back into the lift lobby where they didn't have to wait long for a lift. Back in their own rented penthouse apartment opposite, they discussed the situation while they quickly packed their belongings and changed out of the disguises.

'I've seen his father being interviewed, and that sounded like him.'

'No doubt about it,' Jim replied. 'We'd better disappear before all hell lets loose.'

The sound of sirens hit them as they left the building and made their way to the station.

Chapter 10 – The Path to Heaven

Claire noticed the strong feeling of love which was increasing by the second, and knew they were getting nearer. She recognised that this must be the overwhelming feelings those lucky dead souls who were taken straight there without having to prove themselves in another body on earth experienced. Having almost been in the clutches of Satan himself, this love was the flip side of what she'd felt there, but just as overpowering. She smiled as the memories of her own life hit her, each one an explosion of love and happiness. One moment she was a baby, wrapped in a loving embrace with her grandmother and mother smiling down at her; the next, a child, sitting on her father's lap as he sang, *What a Wonderful World,* only for her. She could almost smell the earthy soil from the garden as she heard the words of the song, as clear as if her father was travelling with her. Then it was as if someone had pressed the fast-forward button. She was a teenager, sitting on the grass, the sun warming her skin and her brothers larking about and joking. Raphael looked at the expression of serenity on his lover's face and guessed what was happening.

'Don't go there, Claire,' he said. 'Concentrate on the here and now.'

'It's lovely, Raphael. I was surrounded by love in the physical world, without realising it at the time. My life was short, but worthwhile.'

'Of course it was, and I know it's hard to focus on others when the memories are so overpowering, but we're their guardians and have a job to do.'

'You're right,' she replied, remembering that she'd been trusted by Amanda and the Committee to do this job and that she was jointly in charge of the safe delivery of two souls. Determined to prove she could do this, Claire gave herself a talking to, but there was still a large part of her that wanted to feel the other lovely memories.

Satisfied for the moment, Raphael knew that Claire would need to muster all of her concentration and willpower to overcome the challenge that was about to present itself. He tried not to think about it as they carried on with their journey.

As they neared Ron and Sandy's final destination, Claire looked at her partner in death and his now soulmate. Their eyes were closed and there were expressions of pure bliss on their faces; they also looked serene and relaxed. Claire smiled as she felt the happiness, warmth, and joy of all the good things that had happened to every soul who passed through the universe. This time it was too much. Overwhelmed by the powerful feelings, she looked at Raphael, smiled, and was about to close her eyes when she saw something in his that stopped her. Whatever it was, Raphael was concerned.

'Stay with me, Claire. Keep your eyes open.'

'It's so wonderful, Raphael, like nothing I've ever felt before. I just want to…'

'You have a choice, Claire. It's not your turn but you're free to go with Ron and Sandy if you want.'

'It's wonderful. Will you come with me Raphael? We can both go. Will we still be together forever?'

'I can't go, my beautiful angel. You'll have to go alone. But your nan's there and you'll know other souls who've been good too.' He took a breath and closed his eyes for a second. Raphael still found it hard to resist but he knew he was needed to help with the fight against evil. He wasn't quite sure what he'd do if she decided to accompany Ron and Sandy.

'It's time to decide, Claire.'

Her eyes were now closed, and she looked the most beautiful he'd ever seen her. Raphael wasn't sure

167

that he was still getting through to her - then Claire opened her eyes.

It was a wonderful experience, but she realised that the supreme ecstasy was also the biggest temptation she had encountered either in life or death, and if she wanted to stay with Raphael, Claire had to fight it. She made up her mind. 'I'm not going anywhere without you.'

'Are you sure?' He tried not to let his relief show but could see by her eyes that it had.

'Absolutely. This is all new to me and I wasn't. But now you've put things into perspective, I know. I want to come here, Raphael, but only if we can be together. If you have work to do before that happens, then so do I. But, God willing, sometime in the future...'

She let the words trail off and there was no need to say anything further. They made their way to the entrance. Nobody was waiting to take in the new souls which surprised Claire.

'Once we let them go they'll simply float away and their most loved ones will appear and guide them.'

'What if nobody loved them in life.'

'Everyone who comes here is loved. Even those lost or weak souls who have come good in the end. But some have more to prove than others in the physical world, and they don't know they're loved until they're on this final journey. You can imagine how those former lost souls feel when that realisation hits them.'

She couldn't imagine feelings more intense and overpowering than those she'd experienced on their way here. 'And what happens then? Will they always feel like this?'

'And then, Claire, all they'll know is love and happiness. It is heaven, after all.'

They watched as Ron and Sandy disappeared into the distance. Their lights became smaller and smaller until eventually, they disappeared for eternity.

Chapter 11 – The Real World

The summer holidays had started and the Director had stopped the courses at the school a month earlier. He planned to restart them at the new facility in Oxford Street, London, in October, a month after the new term would have normally started. The government had already announced that the facility the public knew as a high security prison for the criminally insane was to close, and the remaining prisoners had already been transferred to another secure facility in the south of England. There had initially been an outcry when one of the opposition politicians wrote a newspaper article about overcrowding in prisons, and prisoners being able to have too many freedoms in many locations. The Home Secretary had worked hard to remind the public that this particular facility was, in fact, high security, and that the criminally insane were carefully supervised, did not enjoy freedoms the same as those at open prisons, and there had never been any riots or escapes from there.

The Director and his staff had been given a small suite of rooms to use at the Ministry of Defence in London until their new HQ was up and running and that was the temporary operations base. So many people worked at the MOD that members of the public took little notice of the comings and goings and this would enable the Director and his staff to hide in plain sight if required.

He was no longer worried about security threats or exposure of the old facility's true purpose to the press. Andrew Robertson had been interviewed by a presenter on the TV Show, *Morning World,* following the death of his son. Although consumed with grief, he'd told the presenter that the former high security prison in Glenmalvern was actually a secret training establishment for special forces personnel, and that the

British government had hidden its purpose from the public for a number of years. He also implicated Sir Paul Field in his theory of the deception.

'Paul Field owns the surrounding land and most businessmen would have developed it long before now.'

'Didn't Sir Paul outbid you for that land some years ago, Andrew?' the presenter asked.

'Yes, but that's nothing to do with…'

'And also more recently for the area in London where his new department store, Sunnyfields, will shortly open?'

'Yes, but any entrepreneur worth his salt would have built on that land and I resent the implication that…'

'And hasn't Sir Paul outbid you for a project in Yorkshire involving…'

'I'm not listening to this nonsense anymore,' Andrew responded, pulling the small microphone from his jacket and leaving the studio in a huff.

The Director and Violet chuckled when they watched the replay, knowing that most viewers would believe Andrew Robertson had a personal vendetta against Sir Paul or that his comments were the ramblings of a grief-stricken man. The accusations therefore held little credibility or interest for the majority, and in any case, he wasn't completely accurate in his assumptions. The few journalists who did decide to take a look for themselves found nothing of interest and soon moved on to the next so-called scandal.

Everyone was busy. The twins had returned from France two days before having not found Christina, despite extensive searches which had come to nothing. They'd all met at the school, decided what had to be done, allocated jobs and gone their separate ways for a few days before visiting the school for one final time later in the week to do the final checks of their areas before the formal handover to the landowner, Sir Paul Field, who the public thought had recently bought the land after the facility had closed.

Jim and Tony were spending a few days in the MOD offices trying to track down Christina before their summer holidays – the latest tip-off was that she had travelled to the UK but they hadn't yet discovered her location. Basil was helping Violet in the first phase of potential recruit selection for future courses. Marion was still at the building in Scotland, having been volunteered to take an inventory of the equipment in the old school and to make the final decisions about what to take with them and what should be left behind. Fiona was house hunting, checking out suitable areas down south for all of them to live. They were looking for a location within a reasonable commuting distance, but also in a semi-rural area. Having lived in the beautiful and spacious highlands of Scotland, none of them wanted to become city dwellers again. They had agreed that once she had scoped two or three areas, Marion would join her for the actual house viewings.

All was going to plan, but Christina was about to ruin it.

*****

The baby was strapped to Christina's chest, sleeping peacefully with no idea of the chaos that was about to come as her mum walked towards the perimeter fence. Two days before, she'd seen Tony and his brother talking to a woman who was already in the building, and could tell from their body language, even at a distance, that they were close. Christina hoped the older woman was their mother which would mean she was Eva's Oma. Even if she wasn't, after what Christina had to tell her, she hoped the older woman would do the right thing.

172

To any onlookers, it would seem that she was mad as she walked along, chuntering to herself. The pounding in her head was worse than usual, a sure sign that Witch wanted dominance. Christina was talking to her and trying her hardest to stop the woman from taking over her body and mind. She knew things were getting worse but had made a decision, and it had been the hardest of her life.

She hardly knew him and could only hope that he would love and cherish Eva – after all, she was his daughter. Christina had wanted to cherish her last hours with Eva, but, as usual, Witch was trying her best to scupper her plans. Although exhausted after giving birth, she was pleasantly surprised to find that she was able to block the demon spirit. Christina had started to hold out hope that the bitch had finally left and that she would have a chance to live the rest of her life in peace, as she had always wanted. However, two days ago her peace was shattered when the other voice returned.

'Can't get rid of me that easily…' Witch had chirped in out of nowhere.

Christina had become so used to only having only her own voice in her head that it had literally made her jump, and now she knew what she had to do so her child would have the chance of a normal life – something she had never had.

She planned to get past both guards to get into the building and leave Eva with the older woman, asking her to give her to Tony. If the woman refused to take the baby, Christina would leave her anyway and do a runner. She had quickly realised the flaw in this plan. Even if she could run faster than the woman (which she knew without checking that she could), one of the guards would likely catch her. She therefore intended to put the guards out of action for a while. Taking the tranquilizing needle out of her bag, she carefully filled it with the fast-acting drug Midazolam.

173

The sedative would send the guards to sleep for a few hours and they'd likely wake up with a headache, but there wouldn't be any long-term damage.

Witch was waiting patiently for Christina to carry out her work. Her plan was slightly different, but also involved disabling both guards so she didn't intend to take over just yet.

Christina held the needle behind her back as she neared the fence. She was surprised to see that the outer gate was open, unaware that all operations had concluded at the school. The guard was smoking a cigarette and facing the building. He seemed to be scrutinising the items that were outside, waiting to be collected, Christina assumed. A number of mattresses were stacked neatly, their bases a little further along beside wardrobes and bedside cabinets. *So people had definitely lived here*, she thought, and doubted that that criminally insane would have had so much in their rooms. She remembered what Andre had told her about the facility, and his big plan to be the man to expose the lie and discredit the British Government.

While the guard was preoccupied, she walked through the gate unchallenged. He turned, surprised when she spoke. 'Hello, I wonder if you can help me, please?'

'Oh, hello, love. I think you've come to the wrong place. This is all closed up now and it doesn't look like you're here to help with the furniture removals.' He chuckled to himself.

Christina laughed with him and the guard smiled at the beautiful woman who had appeared from nowhere. The needle was totally unexpected. 'What the hell?' he asked, as she thrust it in his thigh. He said nothing else as he slumped to the ground fighting to stay conscious. She knew the sedative would take a few minutes to take effect and although the man looked sleepy and confused, he was still awake. She also knew he was capable of calling out for help so quickly tied a ribbon around his mouth. He struggled and she could see the panic in his eyes. Whatever Christina did, she wasn't a killer and wanted him to know this.

'Please, don't be frightened. You'll sleep for a few hours but then you'll be okay. Nobody's going to hurt you. Trust me.' She didn't recognise the irony of her words, telling him that nobody was going to hurt him even though she had done just that.

His breathing slowed even though he was still fighting to stay awake. He lost his struggle less than five minutes later when he fell sound asleep, breathing heavily.

He was too big to move so she didn't try. She refilled the needle, walked around him and headed for the main door of the building.

'Well done. I'm impressed,' said Witch.

'Shut up,' Christina answered.

The demon laughed in her head and Christina resisted the urge to argue.

The door opened as she arrived at it and she wasn't sure if she, or the second guard, was the most surprised.

'Hello,' said Christina, 'I'm sorry to bother you but…'

He'd seen a photograph of her and her boyfriend, but as was usual when she met strangers, the man was taken by her beauty and this gave her a few seconds advantage.

'I'm on your side, love,' he said, 'You shouldn't be here…' Then he gasped in shock and looked down at his leg where she'd just thrust the needle.

'I'm so sorry. It's not personal and it'll wear off in a few hours. It's not like anything worse is going to happen to you.' Christina said.

'He's one of ours,' the Witch said, and Christina tried to ignore the vicious pounding in her

175

head, signalling that Witch was fighting for dominance, despite Christina's best efforts to stop her.

'Shut up!' Christina said, as the man staggered to the wall and leant against it, all the while staring at the beautiful mad woman who'd injected him. He knew he should raise the alarm so they wouldn't suspect he'd sold information to the woman's late boyfriend, but why would she do this? His foggy brain reminded him there was nothing classified left in the building – stationery supplies, furniture and machinery, but any information that would have been of interest to the public or those who suspected the real purpose of the building, had already left. With one hand on the wall he managed to take the walkie talkie off his belt.

'Why?' he asked her just before he dropped the radio and joined it by slumping to the floor a few seconds later.

Christina left him there and looked around. Her plan was still to leave Eva with her grandmother and to get out of the building as soon as she could.

'Good job,' said Witch, who was coming through more frequently and stronger. Christina had to fight even harder so she could complete the job. Her daughter's future depended on her winning the fight for now, so she had to stay strong.

Witch knew how much she was struggling. 'There's no point, you know I'm going to win,' she tormented her. 'And when I do, you're going to pay for going against my wishes.' She forced her hand up towards the back of Eva's neck.

'No!' Christina screamed. 'You're not going to hurt her; I won't let you.'

'Do you think you have a choice, Christina? I told you not to have the brat, that it would ruin everything, but you didn't listen and look at us. The brat ruined our body, you've gone mad and it's not the same.'

176

Terrified that Witch would make her hurt Eva, Christina made her way around the building, looking in every room until she found who she was looking for. Each room had a key in the lock and a piece of paper stuck to the door. Some of the papers had the word *clear* written on them with a date underneath, and the others were blank. Those with the blank papers still needed work to be done in the rooms.

Since her reappearance two days before, Witch came and went, but she was staying for longer each time and Christina knew she didn't have much time left before the demon took over her head and body completely. She'd warned she would do this as Christina's punishment for having the baby and had been threatening to *deal with* Eva, each time she returned. Christina was terrified she would carry out her threat and the worst would happen.

Chapter 12 – The Second Test

'Well done, Claire,' Amanda said to her son's soulmate. 'That's one of the hardest tests you will ever have to endure, and many before you have failed. Even the Committee are relieved when angels return after their first time. You've proved to us that you're as strong as we suspected, and you and Raphael are true soulmates as well as a great team.'

Claire tried not to look smug and gave herself a metaphorical pat on the back, but she also wondered why Amanda had said *one of the hardest tests*. Surely, nothing in her future could be as difficult as turning down an opportunity to go to heaven for eternity?

It wouldn't be long before she discovered the reason why.

'You and Raphael must go now, to face your next challenge. Take a host of ten others with you and be strong, child; remember that you can't change that which is preordained.'

Claire wondered what was in store for her. The number of angels Amanda had allocated to accompany them meant they could expect a battle, and she looked at Raphael for guidance. He looked as confused as she did. Her stomach knotted; she felt like she was inside a washing machine, spinning out of control. She tried to get a grip as Amanda continued speaking, 'Good luck and God speed.'

Raphael took her hand and they were off, the host following closely.

'We're at the school,' Claire said, sometime later. 'Who's she?' she asked, before zooming in on the woman with a baby strapped to her chest. 'Wow, she's a stunner.' She shivered and pulled back before whoever was in the woman noticed her presence.

'I have no idea,' said Raphael. 'And yes, she is. I can see you felt the presence too.'

178

'It's a strong one,' Claire replied. 'I've got a feeling this one's going to be hard work.'

'You're right, but there's got to be more to it than this. You've done lots of these Claire; it's almost second nature to you,' he said, looking thoughtful. 'Let's take a look around, see if that sheds some light on the situation.'

They scanned the building, noticing the two unconscious men.

'She's up to no good,' said Claire, stating the obvious. 'Oh, there's my mother. I wonder… Oh, no, Raphael! I hope nothing happens to my mother. She hasn't had enough time with Basil and… Tell me she's going to be okay_'

'I can't tell you anything, Claire. This is all a puzzle to me too, I have no idea what's going to happen.'

'I need to find the twins, see if they're near so they can help Mum if needed.' She flapped her wings frantically in an attempt to calm herself, but also warming up for a speedy flight to wherever she needed to go.

Raphael put a hand on Claire's arm in attempt to calm her. 'Remember what my mother said about that which is preordained?' he said. 'I think you're being tested to accept that which will happen, without trying to change events you have no say in.'

'But she's my mother, Raphael! How can I watch without doing anything? Surely the Committee must understand that?'

'I don't have all the answers, Claire, but I do know that you're not God, and while we're permitted to help sometimes, at others we have to let fate take its course, no matter how hard.'

Claire gave a little cry as she watched the woman with the baby approach the room where her mother was working. Knowing the strength of the evil

179

spirit within the new mother, it was clear there wasn't going to be a happy ending to this situation.

*****

Marion heard footsteps approaching along the corridor and assumed that Bill, one of the security staff, was coming for a chat. She sighed. She'd have a quick word, just to be polite, then carry on with the work. The sooner she finished here, the sooner she could join Basil for an early dinner, then tomorrow, travel down south to meet Fiona who'd phoned to say she'd found a few promising properties in Surrey. Marion put down the inventory she was checking and turned.

'Oh!' she exclaimed, seeing Christina. 'And who might you be?'

The young woman who was standing in front of her took the key out of the door and entered the stationery store.

'Chris…ti…na.'

She was obviously having some trouble communicating and Marion could see she was in the throes of some sort of internal struggle. Her own motherly instincts kicked in. 'What's wrong, my dear?'

Sweat was forming on Christina's brow and she was shaking. 'Listen carefully, I don't know how much time I've got before she takes over.'

'Before who takes over?' Marion asked, adding, 'You're shaking, Christina. Here sit down.' She pulled out the only chair in the room and looked around to see whether she could get past the young woman if required. She was still shaking, and something was very wrong.

'Let me go and get you a drink of water and then we can talk,' said Marion, with the intention of bringing one of the guards back with her.

'No time,' said Christina. 'My baby, Eva. She's your granddaughter.'

Marion shook her head. The woman was clearly delusional and probably on something even with a baby to look after. *Irresponsible to say the least*, she thought. She also wondered how she had got into the building past the two guards without her being alerted. But her current concern was for the child. 'Look, I'm happy to help you if I can, but let's try and keep a grip on reality. Now what do you want from me?'

Christina unstrapped Eva. 'I'm not taking anything. I'm..._there's another woman...' She struggled, wondering how to explain and knowing that this woman wouldn't believe her if she did tell the truth. It was so important for Eva's Oma – under stress, she reverted to her native Dutch, though her own Oma had given her no comfort at any time in her life – to know she was telling the truth. She tried another tack. 'I had a one-night stand with your son, Tony. He doesn't know that Eva's his daughter.'

'No, my son's not...' Marion stopped herself and looked once more at the distressed woman in front of her. Even though she looked pale and unhealthy, with dark circles under her eyes and a drawn face, her beauty was very obvious. She was tall, striking, and her lovely figure showed through the baggy clothes she was wearing. Tony was only human, and Marion knew he missed Libby, despite what she'd done to him. He might well have slept with this woman if she'd offered him comfort and a temporary escape from his loneliness.

'What happened? I mean, how did you meet? What were the circumstances?'

'No time. Just believe me she is your granddaughter. The other woman is coming, you have to get away. Save Eva! Please don't let her hurt Eva.'

'Of course.' Whatever she personally believed, Marion was convinced that the woman, Christina, believed she had another person in her head. *Perhaps*

181

she's schizophrenic? Marion jumped into action. She held out her hands and took the baby. Eva stirred slightly and opened her eyes. She looked up to her grandmother and smiled, and Marion saw the mouth and nose of her twins when they were small babies, albeit a female version. She was now convinced that Christina was telling the truth. 'I'll get some help,' she said. But the woman jumped up from the seat before Marion reached the door and blocked her way.

'Not so fast, Oma,' she said.

Marion had no idea what the word *Oma* meant, but assumed it was an insult from the way the woman said it. Her voice had changed, and she believed the second personality had taken over as Christina had worried it would. *She's probably forgotten to take her medication,* Marion thought. Whatever the reason, this other woman was nasty and could well be dangerous. Marion looked around trying to work out an escape route. She shrugged mentally, telling herself not to be so stupid. She would be calm and patient and reason with her. First, she had to find out what the other personality wanted from her.

'Why don't you sit down, and we can talk about this,' she said, adding, 'and what you want from me.' She put on her most sympathetic expression, though she didn't feel any sympathy at all.

'Okay,' the woman said, but before she sat down, she put the key in the lock and turned it, then removed the key and put it in the pocket of her baggy jacket. They were now locked inside, and Marion tried to suppress the increasing sense of unease, slowly turning to fear, that was building up inside her.

'I didn't want the brat,' she started conversationally. 'Your son was too easy but a good lay and quite talented, even though I say so myself.'

'I don't think I need to know that,' said Marion. The woman was obviously a tart and she tried to hide her distaste.

'I bugged his house like Andre asked me to, but your boys are very clever…' She leaned forward. 'Aren't they, Oma? Tony, or his brother, found one of the bugs shortly after and Andre didn't like it. There again, Andre didn't like a lot of things that happened. And they tried to get us into trouble! Shame he's no longer with us,' she said, studying her fingernails for a moment.

As she watched her, Marion noticed a change beginning. Her expression switched from cruel and confident to panicked.

'Get out and save Eva, while you still can.'

Marion recognised it as the first voice, the original Christina as she thought of her. But as quickly as the voice had appeared, it disappeared, and the second woman was back.

'As I was saying before I was so rudely interrupted,' she said. 'Andre is no longer with us and I'm happy to be back on my own again. Christina disobeyed me once too often and has outlived her usefulness. Literally.' She gave a wicked little laugh. 'I have work to do and a journey to complete, and you and the brat are coming with me.'

'The only place we're going is outside. Now unlock the door and…'

Marion was shocked into silence as the woman picked up some paper, took a lighter out of her pocket and lit it. She threw it into a stack of paper in the corner of the room, which ignited. Plastic folders and poly pockets were next to the papers and they caught fire seconds later.

Marion tried to ignore the initial flames knowing she had to get the key from this woman so she

183

could get out of the room with her granddaughter, and get help to put out the fire.

Witch taunted her by dodging and weaving, and as the woman laughed and wasted time, other items caught light and it wasn't long before they were surrounded by flames. There was a sizzle, followed by an explosion; *the cleaning fluids in the cans,* thought Marion, now becoming desperate. She covered the baby's head with one hand and lunged at the woman. Witch responded by landing a heavy slap to Marion's face. The flames were dancing closer to them and Marion knew this was her last chance to get to the door. The younger woman was stronger but, fuelled by adrenaline and the desire to get the baby to safety, Marion moved quickly and caught the woman by her jacket, stopping her from moving for a second. Witch was surprised and tried to push Marion away. Limited in what she could do with the baby dangling at her front, Marion tried her best to hold on, knowing she had to get the key in order to escape the room.

The flames were now licking up the walls and the ceiling had caught fire. Both women were now concentrating on their struggle. The demon summoned her strength, giving Marion an almighty push. As the momentum of the push threw Marion to the other side of the room, there was an almighty crash. She could only watch as part of the burning ceiling came crashing down onto the mother of her granddaughter, and the woman screamed in agony before passing out.

Marion coughed and looked down at Eva. The baby had been crying up until now, but the cries had weakened and had now stopped altogether. Marion knew they had little time to get to safety. Even if the door had been unlocked, they wouldn't have been able to get to it now through the flames; the only other option was the window. Marion looked out first without opening it, knowing that as soon as it was opened the increased oxygen in the room would accelerate the flames. Looking down, she could see the stack of mattresses but didn't think she'd have a chance of hitting them. She had to make a choice: die in the stationery store of severe burns or smoke inhalation, or jump out of the window and probably die of her injuries? At least that way there could be a chance for the baby. She looked at Eva then closed her eyes for a nano-second, trying to summon the courage, knowing what she had to do.

The flames licked at her legs as she opened the window, as if they were hungry for another victim. Marion climbed quickly out onto the ledge and turned so her back was to the front of the building. She turned her head, trying to judge where the mattresses were, then let go, keeping her arms around the baby, trying to protect her.

*****

Tony was driving the car up to their homes in Scotland so that he and his brother could collect the things they didn't want the packers to take. Jim was in the passenger seat and Fiona in the rear, watching the world go by. The sensation struck and Jim turned the radio off and looked at his brother. Without saying a word, Tony instantly knew that his brother had the awful feeling too.

'I'll phone for an ambulance,' Jim said, and Fiona's ears pricked up.

'An ambulance? What for?'

Tony indicated to exit the motorway, taking the turn for the school instead of heading home.

'What's happened and why are we going this way?' Fiona asked.

'It's Mum,' the twins answered in unison.

'She's in trouble,' Tony added, while his brother took one of the burner phones out of his rucksack and made the call.

185

'Ambulance please, yes the hospital in Glenmalvern,' Jim said, looking at Tony who shrugged his shoulders. 'There's been an accident…Not sure, but it's life and death. Hurry please.'

Fiona listened in morbid fascination. One thing about her husband, he still had the capacity to surprise her after all of their time together. She waited until he'd finished the call before speaking.

'Can one of you please tell me what's going on?'

Jim took the sim card out of the phone and cut it in two. He spoke as he broke the rest of it up and put it in a plastic bag along with bits and pieces of other phones. It would be difficult to explain how they'd known their mum was in trouble, so the best thing was that the call was untraceable.

'We know Mum's had some sort of accident, Fi.'

'But how?'

'Remember how I told you that we both just knew when Claire died? Well I had a feeling about Mum a few minutes ago and Tony had the same.'

'You knew just by looking at each other? She shook her head, glancing out of the window as she did so. Her head stayed in that direction. Oh my God! Look at that smoke. Looks like it's coming from…'

'…the school,' Tony said, flooring the accelerator. They were still a way out but the school was the only building for some miles, so it was obvious to them all.

The sound of loud sirens could be heard within the next few seconds and Tony pulled in to let an ambulance pass on the narrow road. A few minutes later he had to do the same for two fire engines which went screaming by.

'She's going to be all right,' said Fiona, trying to convince herself as much as the twins that her

186

mother-in-law would survive whatever had happened to her. It didn't occur to her for one second that the twins might be wrong about their mother being in danger.

*****

Claire felt like she was watching a horror movie as her mother launched herself off the windowsill and landed on the mattresses. Her body was twisted at an awkward-looking angle and, as the baby screamed in protest, Raphael spoke to her, 'You go to your mother, Claire, and I'll deal with the demon.'

'Be careful, Raphael,'

'I have the host with me, Claire. We'll be fine.'

Claire snapped into action and her surroundings changed from that of the physical world to another dimension. She saw her mother.

Marion wondered if she was dreaming when she saw Claire in the distance. Her daughter was looking at her, surrounded by a beautiful white light. 'Claire!' she called, 'Oh, my beautiful, darling daughter. Look at you! You have wings! I always knew you were an angel.'

Claire smiled. Her mother was in a golden tunnel, its smooth walls giving the impression that light radiated all around her. Her soul hadn't yet left her body. *There's a chance it might not be her time.* She so wanted to hold her and to feel her mother's love, like she had when she'd taken Ron and Sandy to heaven. She held out her arms for her mother to enter, knowing there was no way back if Marion accepted the embrace.

The distance between them closed as Marion started to move towards her. 'Am I dead, Claire? I have a granddaughter and I'd like to see her grow. I love you, Claire, but I don't want to die yet.'

'A granddaughter?' With a will of iron, Claire dropped her arms and her mother stopped moving.

187

'Yes, the baby I held when I jumped. She's Tony's daughter. The mad woman told me and when I looked at Eva, I just knew, Claire.'

'You're a hero, Mum. You saved Mel on your wedding day and now your own granddaughter. You've given her the gift of life, and the chance to live it to the full.'

'I am dead then?'

Claire moved to the tunnel and gently touched her mother's face. Marion lifted a hand to hold her daughter's. The peace and warmth was almost overwhelming for Marion who smiled and closed her eyes, happy to float away to wherever destiny took her.

Claire rapidly withdrew her hand and Marion opened her eyes as the beautiful feeling was snatched from her. 'You don't have to die, Mum. You can fight, it's your choice. What do you want to do?'

'I want to live, darling.'

'Then you can do this. Fight, Mum! Fight with everything you have to save your own life!'

The expression on Marion's face changed and Claire saw the determination in her mother's eyes as an invisible force pulled her back and she disappeared from the tunnel.

*****

'She's back,' shouted a paramedic to his colleague. 'We've got a pulse!'

Neither looked up as Tony skidded the car to a halt as near to the ambulance as he could get, and they all jumped out.

'It's like a war zone,' Jim said, briefly taking in the chaos around them as they rushed towards the paramedics, with Fiona hot on their heels.

'What happened? Is she going to be all right?' asked Jim. When one of the paramedics glanced at him, he added, 'We're her sons.'

188

'Your mother's had a very serious fall,' the medic replied, without looking up again. 'Looks like a head injury and other broken bones. But we've stabilised her, for now. Give us some space to do our job, please.'

They stepped back and watched as Marion was loaded into the ambulance on a gurney. 'We'll follow,' Tony said, and they hurried back towards the car. 'Fiona can you…?'

'I'll stay and make the calls. She's in the best hands now and I'm sure she'll come through this,' she added, hoping her words would give some comfort to her husband and his brother. 'I'll be with you as soon as I can,' she called, as they slammed the car doors and sped off behind the ambulance.

First, Fiona ordered a taxi, and then her next call was to Basil. It was the hardest call she'd ever had to make. 'There's been an accident and Marion's on the way to hospital, Basil.'

'What? What's happened? Which hospital?'

She gave him the details, adding, 'But they're not yet sure of the extent of her injuries. A taxi should be outside for you any time now. I didn't think you'd want to drive.'

'It's here now,' he said. 'I'm going.'

As she watched the fire fighters doing their job, Fiona saw another ambulance and a paramedic passing a screaming baby to one of the medics. She briefly wondered why a baby would be at the school, and who it belonged to, but decided to find out more after she'd phoned the Director. The call was brief.

'I know about the fire and the accident, Fiona, and I'm on my way. So are the police as we can expect to get a lot of the media nosing around. Violet's gone straight to the hospital,' he added.

*****

189

By the time Jim and Tony reached the hospital, Marion had already been triaged.

'She has a bleed on the brain and a broken femur and is in Theatre,' they were informed by a kindly nurse. 'Come with me. You can wait in here.' She took them to a family room and showed them where they could get refreshments, though it was the last thing on their minds.

'Is she going to be okay?' Jim asked.

'We're doing all that we can, and we'll let you know as soon as she comes out of Theatre.'

'Standard response,' Tony said as the nurse left them to it. 'I guess it's touch and go and we just have to play the waiting game.'

Jim sat down and tapped his fingers, wondering how long they'd have to wait until they knew the fate of their mother.

Then they exchanged glances before Jim looked upwards and said, 'You're back then? Is it bad news?'

Both held their breath waiting for their sister's response.

'I certainly am,' said Claire, 'and no, it's not bad news. Mum's not going to die…'

'But her injuries? And the nurse just said…'

'She died briefly at the school but she's back with you now, and as well as wanting to live to spend time with Basil and both of you, she has a new reason to fight for her life.'

The twins sighed with relief. Though still extremely worried, they had no reason to doubt their sister and, despite the information from the medics, knew their mother would live.

'Will she make a full recovery?'

'I can't answer that, Tony. But I do know she'll do everything she can so she can watch her granddaughter growing up.'

'Granddaughter? What are you talking about, Claire? I'd know if Fiona was pregnant…'

'Not your daughter, Jim.'

'But that would mean…' Tony said.

'This is going to come as a shock, Tony. But you have a daughter. Her name is…'

'What?' he interrupted. 'There must be some mistake, Claire…' but even as he was saying the words, Tony's brain was working overtime and he knew it could only be the woman he'd met at the DIY shop and slept with. The same woman who was the girlfriend of Andre Robertson, and most probably the woman who had murdered him. He stopped himself from denying anything and said to Claire, 'Go on.'

'Her name is Eva and she's about two weeks old. Mum nearly killed herself trying to save Eva, Tony. She would rather have died than see her granddaughter die in a fire. She's a proper hero.'

There was silence for a full ten seconds, while the twins tried to take in everything Claire had told them.

'So how do we know that the baby's definitely mine?' he asked. 'And what about the mother?'

'You need to listen very carefully to what I'm about to tell you. The baby's mother was a good woman, but she had some issues with a bad soul. A demon of a bad soul actually, who, it seems, didn't want her to have the baby and decided to punish her for it when she did. The mother wanted to save her child. During the struggle with the demon, and with Mum, she lost her life in the fire.'

'Christina, the woman I…? You mean she set fire to the school?'

'Yes. After tranquilising both guards who were on duty, she found Mum, started a fire, and tried to kill them.'

'What the…'

'Yes, indeed.'

'And you think she was a good woman? How can you say that? And how, exactly, do you know that I'm the baby's father, Claire?'

'Mum is convinced that you are because Eva looks exactly like you both did at the same age, and also the timing is from when you_'

'So you and Mum have actually spoken and_'

The door opened and Basil entered, putting paid to any further discussion about the baby, for the time being.

'Where's Marion? How is she? What happened?' The worry lines on his face made him look ten years older than when they'd last seen him.

Jim put a hand on his forearm. 'Somebody set fire to the school and Mum was trapped in a room. But she jumped out of a window and landed awkwardly on some of the mattresses that were stacked outside. She saved a baby but sustained a head injury and a broken femur, Basil. They're operating on her now.

'Is she going to make it? And what do you mean, saved a baby?'

Tony watched his brother explaining the situation to Basil, his own emotions fraught with both the worry over their mother and the revelation that he was now a father. Some time later the nurse who'd brought them to the family room broke his train of thought.

'The operation was a success. The surgeon managed to stop the bleeding on Marion's brain and she's back on the ward. She's sleeping. You can see her now, but only for a few minutes.'

Chapter 13 – The Afterlife

The witch stayed to watch as Christina's body burned, glad that she had been able to escape the feeling of skin and bone burning in this life. Her only sadness was that she'd had to cut short her stay in the unwelcome host, due to the stupid bitch having a baby. Living in a new mother's mind and body was too draining for most demons, and Witch knew she wouldn't have been able to fully control Christina if she had stayed. She watched the unconscious woman with resentment and hatred, enraged that she had to die so young, forcing her to find another host.

She felt a change in the atmosphere and knew someone was coming. She wasn't close enough to see whether they were bright or dark lights and considered her forthcoming challenge. Would she have to escape the devil's servants, intent on their mission to return her to Hell to face his wrath and punishments beyond her imagination? Or would the angels attempt to take her to the bat cave where she'd spend eternity as a cockroach with no chance of escape?

She decided to enjoy the here and now for a few more moments before attempting to make her escape and, if good fortune was on her side, finding another host to accommodate her needs. She watched as the body in the now inferno took its final breath and Christina's soul departed.

As she rose upwards, the first thing she saw was the orb of darkness.

'Hello, Christina,'

'No! Oh no, no, no!' Christina cried in despair.

As Raphael and the host approached, he heard the dead woman's cries, mingled with the sound of a witch's cackles.

The witch was enraged when she saw them, annoyed that there was no time to have some fun with

Christina in death, as she had in life. She was also afraid. Her strength and fury would help her fight, but even she doubted whether she could overcome the eleven she could see heading towards her.

Watching closely as they neared, the witch quickly picked out the least experienced like a predator seeking its prey – she found the weakest member of the herd, and focussed on him. The young angel didn't know what hit him as a bolt of dark light flew through space and burnt one of his wings. He spun, and tumbled downwards before any of them could smell the burning of singed feathers.

'Mandy, Dylan,' Raphael shouted. 'Save Peter.'

As the angels did as he ordered, there was another shift in the atmosphere. Raphael felt it before the witch and pulled up short, causing the host to stop suddenly behind him. He looked downwards to see more black orbs heading upwards, towards the two souls and towards his fallen angel, Peter, plus Mandy and Dylan who were chasing him. As the demons neared, their natural forms emerged; scarred and ugly faces, cloven feet, gnarled hands, and varied body types; some with scabs hanging off, others leaking rotten blood that filled the space with a putrid sulphur-type smell, even from this distance. As if the sight and smell wasn't enough, they were screaming worse than a thousand caterwauling cats and Raphael knew the situation could only worsen.

He did a swift calculation and made a decision. 'Matthew, prepare everyone and form the circle. I'll be back as soon as I can.'

Matthew began to do as he'd been told, watching as Raphael flew downwards, like a diving Peregrine Falcon. As he did so he blotted the sight of the evils from his mind, replacing it with the memory of the original black orbs he'd first seen. They already had

Peter in their clutches and Raphael knew he only had one opportunity to save the terrified angel. He focussed and relaxed before crashing into them like a bullet. It had the desired effect and the demons dissipated, initially heading back from whence they'd come. Peter had been released and Raphael flapped his wings to stop the momentum of his dive, changing direction, heading towards the distraught junior angel. He gathered him up in his arms as he headed back upwards, meeting Mandy and Dylan on his way.

'Take him back to the host,' he said. 'I'll be with you as soon as I can.'

They encircled Peter and moved quickly, heading for the others.

Raphael knew they were outnumbered and could see the demons were regrouping. He wondered whether he could catch the evil witch before the legion of demons arrived. Raphael was in a space equidistant from the witch, Christina, and his own host, and below them, the demons were gathering speed and getting closer by the second.

The witch was cackling as happily as she knew how, and he could see her tormenting the soul of the woman whose life she had taken prematurely. *She thinks she can escape!* The thought hit Raphael and his sense of logic was replaced by anger over the hell that the witch had made of Christina's life. A hell which was now carrying on into her death. It must seem to the poor soul that her afterlife was going to be as tragic and horrendous as her physical life. His sense of fair play kicked in and he tried his best not to acknowledge his anger, recognising that this was what the witch would want him to be, and knowing that it would strengthen her and weaken him.

He closed his eyes and pictured his beautiful soulmate. He imagined holding hands with Claire, walking along a beach with the sun caressing their skin and the breeze heightening their senses with the slight salty smell of the sea. They laughed together and then they kissed... *That's better.* Now fully prepared, he concentrated, looked towards the sound of the cackling and visualised her true form. In front of him, the dark orb slowly changed shape to an old woman with long, lank, grey hair. Her almost black eyes were hard and cold, set in a face full of wrinkles and a mouth that was turned down into what looked like a permanent droop. She opened it to cackle again, and the few teeth inside were rotten or chipped. Raphael wished he'd not summoned her real image. In contrast, the good soul that she'd tormented was one of the most stunning examples of human beauty that he'd ever set eyes on. The contrast enhanced both the first's ugliness and the other's beauty.

'You're a beautiful angel,' Christina said, in awe of the vision in front of her and able to forget about the awful witch for a moment. 'Can you save me?'

'Yes, I can,' Raphael said.

'Nobody can save you,' the witch screamed in outrage. 'You're going to hell forever, and if you think your life on earth was painful and miserable, look out, princess, that doesn't even come close...'

Christina whimpered and Raphael had heard enough. 'Stop!' he ordered, so loudly that the atmosphere shook like there had been a clap of tremendous thunder. He saw fear in the eyes of the witch for the first time. Not having the time to summon the others, surround her with the circle and gradually change her into a cockroach ready for delivery to the cave, Raphael summoned the little strength he had left. Without warning, he threw a bolt, hoping it would connect and instantly transform her into a cockroach. But her appearance belied a swiftness that he wouldn't have guessed at, and even taken by surprise she almost dodged it. Almost, but not quite. The witch screamed in horror as Raphael and Christina watched her foot change into that of an insect's hook-like tarsus, with claws on the end. It almost suited the evil soul, Raphael thought as he tried to recharge as quickly as possible, knowing he might not win this fight.

The demons were getting closer and decisions had to be made.

The witch knew she didn't have the strength to fight the angel and the Devil's slaves were getting closer. She weighed up her options: she could continue tormenting Christina; or avoid deliverance, either from the demons to Hell, or from the angel, to the cave. She also couldn't bear the thought of being further deformed and knew if she retreated now, she at least had the chance of finding another host and returning to fight this bastard at a later date. However long it took, that would be her main priority; to take revenge for what he'd done to her. As she watched his followers heading towards him, she knew she'd need all her strength to escape and couldn't risk fighting back.

Raphael was pleased that Matthew was bringing the host to help instead of waiting for him to return to them. It gave him a bit more time, and a better chance of success. 'Rescue Christina, the good soul,' Raphael called to his host. 'I'll deal with the witch.'

Events going on around her had given the witch the time she needed, and as the angels approached Christina, she prepared to make her move to disappear into the ether. But for it to work she would have to distract the angel in command. She wracked her brain, watching him as she did so. The witch wasn't overcome by his beauty like Christina had been, but even she recognised his exceptional good looks and wondered. *It's certainly worth a try,* she decided.

'I'm going to escape and I'm going to find your soulmate-and when you see what I've done to her, you'll be sorry you've messed with me. You'll both be sorry.'

Taken aback by her words, Raphael hesitated and it was all the time she needed. She disappeared in a glow of black light.

He resisted the urge to chase straight away. 'Take Christina and the others and look after Peter, he's had a shock,' he said to Matthew. Then, 'Mandy and Dylan, do everything that Matthew says, without question.'

'What about you?' Matthew asked. 'It's not safe on your own and…'

Summoning what was left of his strength, Raphael disappeared in a flash of light before Matthew finished speaking.

He could still see the black orb in the distance but despite using all of his strength it became smaller and smaller and Raphael eventually pulled up, knowing he couldn't catch her. The dive into the demons had taken more out of him than he'd realised, and his priority now was to find Claire and to get them both to safety where they could recuperate before continuing their never-ending fight against all that was evil.

Chapter 14 – A Special Someone

Marion opened her eyes and looked straight at Basil, then across to her sons.

'Hello,' she said, her voice croaky.

Basil picked up a cup of water and held it to her lips. Marion took a tentative sip, then tried to gulp as much as she could.

'Hold on,' said a nurse as she entered the room. She fussed over Marion, checking her vital signs.

'I saw your sister,' Marion told the twins a few seconds later. 'She's an angel.' Then, looking directly at Basil, she said, 'I love you,' before losing the fight to keep her eyes open. Within seconds she was sleeping again.

'I'll tell the doctor she woke up and early indications are that there's little or no brain damage. Looks like Marion will make a full recovery,' the nurse said.

The men collectively sighed with relief.

'And no need to concern yourselves about the *angel* comments. It's perfectly natural for traumatised patients to think they've seen a loved one when they've been brought back from the brink of death.'

'Thank you, nurse,' Tony said, grinning at Jim.

The nurse looked from one twin to the other, and as she left the room, wondered why they found her comment so amusing.

Basil kissed his wife's cheek gently and she smiled in her sleep.

'We'll leave you to it for a while,' Tony said, giving Basil's shoulder a reassuring squeeze. They left the room and knowing her mother was now out of immediate danger, Claire followed the twins into the corridor.

'I can't believe I'm a father,' Tony said, allowing himself to process the information properly now that they knew their mother was going to recover.

'These things happen,' said Jim. 'Shall we go and look?'

Tony looked at his brother in amazement. 'These things happen! These things happen, Jim? I find out our mother died saving a baby who I'm told is my daughter, and the baby's mother – who was most likely a murderer - is dead and is also the reason that our mother is in the intensive treatment unit, and you say *these things happen!* That's the biggest understatement I've ever heard! I just don't know what_'

'Can I help you, gentlemen?' asked the same nurse who'd spoken to them in their mother's room asked.

Tony stopped his rant. 'Can I see Eva now?'

'This way,' she said, and they both followed.

It hit him as soon as her tiny hand gripped his finger. The surge of protective love he felt left him in no doubt that Eva was his daughter. Jim recognised the difference in his brother and knew their lives would change from this day forward.

Eva looked from one man to the other and smiled. Even though her Auntie Claire knew she couldn't see her, she still coochy cooed at her and made funny faces. Claire had the biggest shock of them all when baby Eva's big blue eyes looked directly at her and giggled at her silliness.

'She's beautiful,' said Tony, 'just like her mother. You're a special little girl, aren't you?' he added.

'She certainly is,' said Claire, acknowledging that her brothers had no idea exactly how special Eva already was.

*****

200

The witch knew she had to go into hiding for a while until the demons returned to Hell and the annoying angels stopped trying to find her to turn her into a cockroach. If she had the nature to admit she'd made a mistake, she would have acknowledged that threatening the angel hadn't been her best decision. Too stubborn to acknowledge this, even to herself, she travelled back to the physical world as fast as she could, knowing that lying dormant inside a new-born was the best place to hide, just like she had with Christina. And what better way than to continue punishing Christina for ruining everything.

Toying with how she would explain Eva's gift to Tony and Jim, Claire felt the presence. Even if she hadn't, Eva's instant change from peaceful to stressed would have warned her. She wasn't quick enough, and Claire watched in horror as the demon made to enter Eva.

'What's the matter,' Tony asked his daughter, a worried frown on his face.

Eva screamed in answer, and as Claire prepared herself for a fight to remove the evil from her niece's mind and body, she pulled up short. Eva was still screaming, but not because the evil was now inside her, but because she was repelling her. The evil kept trying to enter the baby over and over again, and to Claire it looked like she was coming up against an invisible wall that she bounced off each time. She had never seen such spiritual strength in one so young and was in awe.

'Claire, what's happening?' Tony was now panic stricken and all the twins could do was to look at Eva struggling with a force unknown to them.

'There's a problem and I'm dealing with it,' Claire told them, trying to understate the seriousness of the situation in order not to frighten or panic them. 'I have to leave you for a little while, but don't worry, Eva will be okay, no matter how much she looks like she isn't.'

Eva let out another scream, and her anguish had the opposite effect of Claire's words on the twins. Tony picked up his daughter, carefully avoiding the wires that were attached to both her and the machine next to her incubator. He whispered words of tenderness as his daughter continued to scream.

The witch was apoplectic. This was a baby less than three weeks old for Devil's sake! How could she possibly rebut her? The madder she got, the harder she tried, and her strength sapped away as she did so.

Seeing that Eva was safe, though anguished, made Claire change her plan. The weaker the evil, the better her chance of successfully getting rid of her once and for all. It was a difficult decision but she allowed the situation to continue while Eva was capable of stopping the evil being from taking over her mind and body.

When the evil became quieter and looked like she was almost spent, Claire felt another presence and smiled. Eva stopped screaming and a strange peace came over her.

'You've got the knack, bro,' Jim told his brother, and Tony puffed up like he'd just won a *Father of the Year* competition, both believing it was Tony's smell and his soothing words that had calmed Eva.

Only Eva, and those on the other side were aware of Raphael's presence. The baby's eyes followed the beautiful new angel as he went to her auntie's side.

'You can't extinguish me!' The witch screamed, apoplectic with rage. 'Who do you think you are? I won't have a black man in charge of my future. I'm going to finish you both_'

Both Raphael and Claire remained calm, despite the insults. They'd long since learned that losing tempers only served to fuel the evils and put them at an

202

advantage. On her own now, against them both, the evil had no chance. Eva's supernatural strength had weakened her, and she had no power left.

'You can't finish me. I won't have it!' she said.

'Let me close Eva's eyes first, Raphael, so she doesn't have to watch,' Claire said, ignoring the insults of the witch.

'It won't make a difference, my love, she's seeing us through her third eye. An extraordinary ability for one so young.'

'We're that sort of family,' said Claire, unable to resist.

He smiled for a second, loving the way she could use humour under the direst of circumstances. Then they both became serious.

'Ready?' he asked. She waggled her wings in answer, then lifted a forefinger.

'Fire!' Raphael commanded and they each threw a bolt of white light towards the witch. The bolts combined mid-air, then hit the witch in her solar plexus. The force of it took her spinning backwards, and by the time she hit the wall in the room, her thighs and chest had already taken the form of a cockroach.

Witnessing the spectacle, Eva let out another scream and started crying again.

'You can't stop…' The witch didn't finish the sentence as first her head and then the rest of her body transformed.

'Quickly,' said Raphael, and Claire joined hands with him to encircle the ugly, squirming insect.

'I have to go,' Claire shouted to her brothers. 'But I'll be back as soon as I can, and everything will be all right now. Look after my precious niece and get that dog of yours to sleep in her room.'

They were on their way to the Bat Cave before Tony or Jim had a chance to respond.

Epilogue

Street lamps lit Oxford Street in the early hours of the morning, and the Director looked up at the impressive new building.

'We have a hot meal for you. Then you can shower and sleep in a warm bed.'

His train of thought broken, he turned to the sound of the voice. A shelter volunteer was talking to a homeless man who was lying in his sleeping bag inside one of the doorways of the department store. The woman managed to talk him into leaving and he watched as they got into a white van and the vehicle disappeared. The ensuing silence was broken by the occasional revellers passing by, but he ignored them, now deep in thought.

The following evening would be pandemonium, with shoppers queuing to see the opening of *Sunnyfields* department store, and to get a glimpse of the charismatic owner, Sir Paul Field who would likely be accompanied by his younger wife, Lady Stacey.

A smile played around the Director's eyes.

If only they knew the real purpose of part of that building.

Acknowledgements

Thanks to my husband Allan, to my awesome editor Jill Turner, and to Jessica Bell for another fantastic cover. Thanks also to all of my friends for their support, especially Julie, Trudy, Su, Tina, Craig, Libby, Jo, and Helen.

Thank you for purchasing this book. If you have time to leave a short review so that other readers can find my books, I'd be extremely grateful.

Another Author's Note

If you enjoyed the Afterlife series, you may be interested in my other books:

Unlikely Soldiers Book 1 (Civvy to Squaddie)
Unlikely Soldiers Book 2 (Secrets and Lies)
Unlikely Soldiers Book 3 (Friends and Revenge)
Unlikely Soldiers Book 4 (Murder and Mayhem)

Court Out (A Netball Girls' Drama)

Zak, My Boy Wonder (non-fiction)

The Island Dog Squad Book 1 (Sandy's Story)
FREE AT THIS LINK
https://dl.bookfunnel.com/wdh6nl8p08
The Island Dog Squad Book 2 (Another Secret Mission
The Island Dog Squad Book 3 (People Problems)

And for children:

Jason the Penguin (He's Different)
Jason the Penguin (He Learns to Swim)

Reindeer Dreams

Further information is on my website
https://debmcewansbooksandblogs.com or you can connect with me on Facebook:
https://www.facebook.com/DebMcEwansbooksandblogs/?ref=bookmarks

About the Author

Following a career of over thirty years in the British Army, I moved to Cyprus with my husband to become weather refugees.

I've written children's books about Jason the penguin and Barry the reindeer, and books for a more mature audience about dogs, the afterlife, soldiers and netball players, along with a non-fiction book about a very special boy named Zak.

'Court Out (A Netball Girls' Drama)' is a standalone novel. Using netball as an escape from her miserable home life, Marsha Lawson is desperate to keep the past buried and to forge a brighter future. But she's not the only one with secrets. When two players want revenge, a tsunami of emotions is released at a tournament, leaving destruction in its wake. As the wave starts spreading throughout the team, can Marsha and the others escape its deadly grasp, or will their emotional baggage pull them under, with devastating consequences for their families and team-mates?

My most popular books are the supernatural suspense Afterlife series. I was in the garden contemplating whether to squash an irritating ant or to let it live. I wondered whether anyone *up there* decides the same about us and thus the series was born. Book six is currently in the planning stage and I'm not yet sure when the series will end.

'The Island Dog Squad' is a series of novellas told from a dog's point of view. It was inspired by the rescue dog we adopted in 2018. The real Sandy is a sensitive soul, not quite like her fictional namesake, and the other characters are based on Sandy's real-life mates.

'Zak, My Boy Wonder', is a non-fiction book co-written with Zak's Mum, Joanne Lythgoe. I met Jo and her children when we moved to Cyprus in 2013. Jo shared her story over a drink one night and I was astounded, finding it hard to believe that a family could be treated with such cruelty, indifference and a complete lack of compassion and empathy. This sounded like a tale from Victorian times and not the twenty-first century. When I suggested she share her story, Jo said she was too busy looking after both children – especially Zak who still needed a number of surgeries – and didn't have the emotional or physical energy required to dig up the past. Almost fourteen years after Zak's birth, Jo felt ready to share this harrowing but inspirational tale of a woman and her family who refused to give up and were determined not to let the judgemental, nasty, small-minded people grind them down.

When I'm not writing I love spending time with Allan and our rescue dog Sandy. I also enjoy keeping fit and socialising, and will do anything to avoid housework.

Printed in Great Britain
by Amazon

44713705R00129